THE LAST
FIRST KISS

What Reviewers Say
About Julie Cannon's Work

Shut Up and Kiss Me

"A feel good, tingly romance…"—*Best Lesfic Reviews*

"Fast-paced, sexy, and fun with a bit of an insta-love plot (a trope I love!). I thoroughly enjoyed this read."—*JK's Blog*

"Great story, and I will definitely read this author again!" —Janice Best, Librarian (Albion District Library)

Wishing on a Dream—*Lambda Literary Award Finalist*

"[The main characters] are well-rounded, flawed and with backstories that fascinated me. Their relationship grows slowly and with bumps along the way but it is never boring. At times it is sweet, tender and emotional, at other times downright hot. I love how Julie Cannon chose to tell it from each point of view in the first person. It gave greater insight into the characters and drew me into the story more. A really enjoyable read."—*Kitty Kat's Book Review Blog*

"This book pulls you in from the moment you pick it up. Keirsten and Tobin are very different, but from the moment they get together, the heat and sexual tension are there. Together they must work through their fears in order to have a magical relationship." —*RT Book Reviews*

Smoke and Fire

"Cannon skillfully draws out the honest emotion and growing chemistry between her heroines, a slow burn that feels like constant foreplay leading to a spectacular climax. Though Brady is almost too good to be true, she's the perfect match for Nicole. Every scene they share leaps off the page, making this a sweet, hot, memorable read."—*Publishers Weekly*

"This book is more than a romance. It is uplifting in a very down-to-earth way and inspires hope through hard-won battles where neither woman is prepared to give up."—*Rainbow Book Reviews*

I Remember

"Great plot, unusual twist and wonderful women. ...[*I Remember*] is an inspired romance with extremely hot sex scenes and delightful passion."—*Lesbian Reading Room*

Breaker's Passion

"...an exceptionally hot romance in an exceptionally romantic setting. ...Cannon has become known for her well-drawn characters and well-written love scenes."—*Just About Write*

"Cannon writes about Hawaii beautifully, her descriptions of the landscape will make the reader want to jump on the first plane to Maui."—*Lambda Literary Review*

"Julie Cannon brilliantly alternates between characters, giving the reader just enough backstory to entice, but not enough to overwhelm. Cannon intertwines the luscious landscape of Maui and it's tropical destinations into the story, sending the reader on a sensuous vacation right alongside the characters."—*Cherry Grrl*

Descent

"If you are into bike racing, you'll love this book. If you don't know anything about bike racing, you'll learn about this interesting sport. You'll finish the book with a new respect for the sport and the women who participate in it."—*Lambda Literary Review*

"Julie Cannon once again takes her readers somewhere many have not been before. This time, it's to the rough and tumble world of mountain bike racing."—*Just About Write*

Power Play

"Cannon gives her readers a high stakes game full of passion, humor, and incredible sex."—*Just About Write*

Just Business

"Julie Cannon's novels just keep getting better and better! This is a delightful tale that completely engages the reader. It's a must read romance!"—*Just About Write*

Unchartered Passage

"Cannon has given her readers a novel rich in plot and rich in character development. Her vivid scenes touch our imaginations as her hot sex scenes touch us in many other areas. *Uncharted Passage* is a great read."—*Just About Write*

Heartland

"There's nothing coy about the passion of these unalike dykes— it ignites at first encounter and never abates. ...Cannon's well-constructed novel conveys more complexity of character and less overwrought melodrama than most stories in the crowded genre of lesbian-love-against-all-odds—a definite plus."—Richard Labonte, *Book Marks*

"Julie Cannon has created a wonderful romance. Rachel and Shivley are believable, likeable, bright, and funny. The scenery of the ranch is beautifully described, down to the smells, work, and dust. This is an extremely engaging book, full of humor, drama, and some very hot, hot sex!"—*Just About Write*

Heart 2 Heart

"*Heart 2 Heart* has many hot, intense sex scenes; Lane and Kyle sizzle across the pages. It also explores the world of a homicide detective and other very real issues. Cannon has given her readers a read that's fun as well as meaty."—*Just About Write*

Visit us at www.boldstrokesbooks.com

By the Author

Come and Get Me

Heart 2 Heart

Heartland

Uncharted Passage

Just Business

Power Play

Descent

Breakers Passion

I Remember

Rescue Me

Because of You

Smoke and Fire

Countdown

Capsized

Wishing on a Dream

Take Me There

The Boss of Her

Fore Play

Shut Up and Kiss Me

The Last First Kiss

THE LAST
FIRST KISS

by
Julie Cannon

2021

ISBN 13: 978-1-63555-768-8

This Trade Paperback Original Is Published By
Bold Strokes Books, Inc.
P.O. Box 249
Valley Falls, NY 12185

First Edition: January 2021

Credits
Editor: Shelley Thrasher
Production Design: Susan Ramundo
Cover Design By Tammy Seidick

Acknowledgments

This is my twentieth book with Bold Strokes, and I could not have done it without everyone who is in front and behind the scenes at BSB. From Rad who took a chance on a first time author years ago, to Sandy who *really* runs the place, to Shelley who makes my stories even better, and everyone who makes Bold Strokes Books the powerhouse in lesbian fiction it has become, I, and our readers, thank you.

Dedication

For all of the women who have had,
or will have, their last first kiss.

CHAPTER ONE

Are you out of your mind? No fucking way." Matt slid the fat, white envelope across the table in front of her. It stopped in front of Becca's half-empty wineglass. Sandra had dashed into the bar a few minutes ago, winded from hustling from her office a few blocks away.

"No and yes, you are. I've already talked with Stephen, and he'll take care of the dog and the house." Stephen was Becca's brother, who lived down the block.

"Jordan's gone to that godforsaken military summer camp he begged you to let him go to, and you haven't had a vacation in forever."

"That's not true," Matt protested. "Jordan and I…" Matt had at least six examples of vacations she and her son had taken in the last few years, but she didn't get a chance to mention any of them.

"A grown-up vacation," Becca said. "Without kids, where you can meet people and have adult conversation."

"And get laid," Sandra interjected.

Sandra and Becca pounced on her like a wrestling tag team. They continued their assault on Matt's denial, and when one ran out of gas and argument as to why she should accept their gift of two weeks at a lesbian resort on a tropical island in the British West Indies, the other jumped in.

"I *am* dating," Matt lied, probably being a bit too emphatic. There was a difference between coffee with someone and having sex. Unfortunately, she wasn't doing either. Since her wife Andrea had died six years ago, the energy-sucking challenges of raising a toddler by herself made any interest in sex a distant memory. But that nugget of information would only fuel their argument.

"Trust us," Sandra said, exchanging knowing looks with Becca. "You need to have more sex than dates."

Matt leaned back in the chair, knowing when she'd been beaten. Both women sitting across from her were attorneys, but never on opposing sides. Sandra was the lead partner of the most prestigious lesbian law firm in the state and was dressed in an expensive red Armani suit that she once described to Matt as her don't-fuck-with-me suit. Her naturally blond hair was in a French braid, her makeup and jewelry expensive but subtle. Her cheekbones were flawless, and she had the natural grace Matt wished she had. Sandra was also filthy rich, as she described it, all family money, but donated a vast amount to various causes each year.

Becca was the complete opposite. First, she was straight and had a serious boyfriend. Barely five feet tall, she carried an extra twenty pounds and was dressed more casually in a pale-blue dress under a white jacket and low black pumps. She had recently been reelected and, at thirty-eight, was one of the youngest district attorneys in the country.

The three of them had met in college their freshman year when they shared a three-bedroom, two-bath dorm room. Becca and Sandra shared a bathroom, and between Sandra's long blond hair and Becca's even longer curly black hair, the plumber was constantly snaking their tub drain. Matt liked to think of them as her girl posse.

"But this is too much," Matt protested, gesturing to the envelope that had somehow ended up back in front of her.

"Nothing's worth more than happiness, Mattie, and we want to help you find it," Becca said.

"And to make sure you do," Sandra jumped in excitedly, her green eyes sparkling, "we're going with you."

Matt gawked at her two friends.

"If we don't, you'll sit in your room and either read a book or write another one," Becca said seriously.

"That's my job." Matt was still stunned from this conversation. After she'd gotten her life back together, she'd started writing children's books. It had always been a dream of hers and gave her time to be with Jordan whenever he needed her, which, until the last year or so, was always. She also wrote lesbian erotica, which was where the big money was. She didn't talk too much about that side of her writing with anyone other than the two women sitting across from her.

"Not for two weeks, it won't be." This time it was Sandra whose voice was firm.

This whole vacation thing had started last week, when her phone rang as she was pulling out of the parking lot after dropping Jordan off at camp.

"Are you bawling like a baby?" *Becca's voice was crystal clear as it came through her car speakers.*

"No. I'm crying like any mother sending her child off to camp for the first time." *She had just dropped Jordan off on the meticulously manicured grounds of the military summer camp, where he'd be for the next eight weeks. Matt knew this was the last she'd see of her little boy, if she ever had a little boy, she thought. Jordan was, at times, a debilitating reminder of his mother. He was a ram-rod straight nine-year-old, who had to have everything in his room in its exact place, insisted on getting his hair cut every five weeks whether or not it needed it, ironed his clothes with military creases, and didn't care what his school peers thought of him.*

She'd managed to hold back tears she knew would embarrass him until she got in the car. He'd insisted on no public displays of affection, so she'd hugged him and smothered him with kisses before they left the house this morning. She'd prepared herself as best any mother could, but the reality was far more painful.

"Come over and we'll get drunk," *Becca said.*

"I've been on the road three hours today and have another three to go."

"Then you'll definitely need a drink."

"What I need to do is go home, suck it up, and start getting used to the silence in the house." When Jordan had started school, the neighborhood kids would often congregate at the Parker house. Matt preferred it that way. She could keep an eye on Jordan and his friends. Kids came and went at her house, their parents staying to chat for a few minutes when dropping off or picking up. But it would be a long, lonely summer.

"You need to have eight weeks of sleepovers," Becca said as Matt turned onto the interstate.

"We've had this discussion, Becca," and she was weary of it. Matt didn't want to get serious with anyone. She did not want to parade different women in and out of Jordan's life until she found Ms. Second Time Around. Because of that preference, she'd been out only a handful of times since Andrea's death. She let her friends believe she was dating and, so far, had evaded having to make any introductions. It wasn't for lack of trying on their part. They were constantly on her about double-dating or bringing a date to a party or barbeque.

"And we're going to continue to have it until you do."

Matt detected more than a little exasperation in her friend's voice. "You don't need to worry about me. My sex life is as full as it needs to be. I've got to go. My mom's calling on the other line. Talk to you soon." Matt had felt slightly guilty about lying to Becca.

"When was the last time you got laid?" Becca asked, pulling Matt away from her memories.

"What?"

"When was the last time you got laid?"

Matt took a deep breath to rein in her temper. "That's none of your business."

"We are your best friends, and it *is* our business." Sandra nodded her agreement.

"I'm not going to talk about this with you two."

"We don't want you to talk about it, Mattie. We want you to do it."

"You've changed, Mattie," Sandra said, suddenly serious. She reached across the small table and took her hand.

The bartender had set another drink in front of her when she'd been daydreaming. Matt looked around at the television monitors, where every station had a different sporting event playing.

"Of course I have," Matt said, hoping to sound disinterested. A niggling feeling started to creep up her neck. "We all have. It's part of growing up and growing old."

"You know we love you," Becca said, glancing at Sandra as if needing support. She nodded.

"Why does this feel like an intervention?" Matt tried to laugh it off but wasn't successful.

"Because it is."

Matt recognized the serious expressions on her friends' faces. They weren't looking at their hands or the floor, but right at her. These women loved her. She wanted to relax but couldn't.

"We love you," Becca said again. "We loved Andrea and think the world of Jordan."

"But…" Matt was anxious for this to be over.

"But you have been living in Andrea's shadow for too long. You need to live your own life. The unrealistic scene the army, Andrea's parents, and even Jordan have laid on you isn't fair. Just because Andrea's life ended, yours doesn't have to. They expect that of you, and it's not right."

Matt saw nothing but concern, understanding, and more than a little truth in Becca's eyes.

"It's time to step out and live your own life, not what others think it should be."

Becca squeezed her hand before continuing.

"Andrea was a giver. A giver of life with Jordan and a saver of life with her patients. And she would not want to keep you from living yours. It's not healthy, and it has to be terribly lonely."

Matt's gut clenched. Becca had hit the proverbial nail on the head. She was busy—with Jordan, her writing, appearances, and all the other single-mom homeowner responsibilities. But late at night, when Jordan was asleep and the house quiet, that well of loneliness threatened to suck her in.

She'd often look at herself in the mirror and wonder what everyone saw. Becca was right. She was under intense pressure to live up to what others thought she should do as the wife of a dead hero. Jordan's understandable but unrealistic idolization of his mother was adding extra weight that she was finding more and more difficult to bear.

Andrea hadn't been perfect. She had flaws, and, Matt had recently admitted to herself that their marriage had been struggling due to her commitment to the army. Matt would never ask Andrea to quit or not go. Being an army nurse was her life, and her death had affected a lot of people.

Now that Jordan didn't need her every moment of every day, the reality and loneliness of her life had started to set in. At times she felt guilty and almost resentful of Andrea's death. Her friends were right. She was too young to continue to live under the ghost of Andrea. The cracks in the façade were starting to splinter.

"We're here for you, Mattie. To support you however you need and to kick you in the ass, which is what we're doing. But don't worry. We won't cramp your style…"

"Or your ability to get laid." Sandra said.

Matt rolled her eyes.

"Or your ability to be *alone*," Becca said, emphasizing the word but with still the same meaning. "We have a three-bedroom suite, and we can giggle and gossip like we did in college."

"I don't even know where we're going." Matt had read the departure date was in ten days and that the final destination on her ticket was Providenciales, but she had no idea where it was.

"Providenciales is one of the islands in Turks and Caicos. It's a territory of the UK and is southeast of the Bahamas. You'll love it there," Becca said.

Matt looked at her friends, who had always supported her. They'd been there for her, helped her pick up the pieces when Andrea was killed, and sat with her when Jordan had a raging fever in the middle of the night. They babysat when she had to go on a book tour and listened to her vent about the unfairness of Andrea dying. They were more than her friends; they were her family.

It would be good to get away for a while. The press was clamoring for a statement, and the *Military Times* was waiting for her comment on the article they'd written about Andrea. She'd read it three times, and it still sounded cold. Her wife had died, for God's sake, and all they were focusing on was that Andrea would be the first open lesbian to be awarded the Medal of Honor. They'd just stated the facts, included no emotion. No mention of the wife and young son she'd left behind when she was killed. Andrea was a vibrant wife and mother, with hopes and dreams for them as a family. Yet the article painted a flat, one-dimensional picture of the thirty-eight-year-old army nurse who had lost her life saving others.

It had been six years since Andrea came home in a gleaming metal coffin covered by the American flag. She was flanked by eight honor guards, the edges of the stars and stripes flapping in the light, afternoon breeze.

Reluctantly Matt took the envelope Becca and Sandra had left and set it on the seat next to her under her phone. She had zero chance of returning it and found that she didn't want to. She needed to get away, out from under the sweltering blanket of her in-laws, her responsibilities of taking care of everyone else before herself. She needed time for herself. Everyone did. She planned to enjoy this vacation to the fullest. Sun, sand, and sex.

"When do we leave?"

CHAPTER TWO

Other than several businessmen typing away feverishly on their laptops, the first-class lounge was nearly empty. Kelly Newsome had arrived in plenty of time for her 8:15 a.m. flight and enjoyed the complimentary breakfast and delicious coffee. She'd traded Suzanne's ticket for an upgrade to first class. She deserved it.

She and Suzanne had planned to spend the next two weeks enjoying everything Providenciales, one of the main islands in Turks and Caicos, had to offer. They had reservations for a jet-ski tour to the adjacent islands, snorkeling in Turtle Bay, trying their skill at kite surfing, wandering the city streets, museums, art galleries, and even taking a day trip to the island of Grand Turks to watch the cruise ships arrive and depart. They'd also talked about making love in the warm sand on a secluded island and a chartered sunset dinner cruise for two.

Along with the hotel, deposits for these other activities had been paid, and when she'd called to cancel, she'd found out they were non-refundable. Kelly had enough to deal with and didn't want to humiliate herself further by begging for a refund because she'd caught the woman she'd been involved with for the past three years having sex with one of her good friends. Or at least she *had* been one of her friends.

"Miss Newsome?"

A beautiful young woman in a crisp airline uniform stood in front of her, an expectant look on her face. Obviously, she'd called her name more than once.

"I'm sorry. Yes?" Kelly said, wrenching her mind back to the present.

"Your flight to Miami will be boarding in a few minutes."

"Thank you."

"Can I get you anything before you board?"

Other than a do-over of the past few years but with a completely different ending, she thought. "No, thank you, Pam," she replied, looking at the gold nametag perched above her perky left breast.

She made a stop in the ladies' room and caught her reflection in the mirror as she washed her hands. Kelly, always on the lean side, had lost more than a few pounds in the past few weeks. She wasn't heartbroken or paralyzed with grief; she simply didn't have much of an appetite. Her shoulder-length blond hair was up in a ponytail, her green eyes sharp but tired. She'd long ago stopped trying to cover the scar on the left side of her neck that ran from just in front of her ear to three inches below her jaw. The bright-red, ugly scar from the stick her brother had thrown at her when she was six had faded to a pale, thin line that, as she got older, would look just like all the other lines in her neck. She was not looking forward to that.

Kelly owned a small women-only electrical company, and as her company grew, her time outdoors had dwindled, but she tried to get out on a site as much as she could. No way could she come back from two weeks on the beach without a spectacular tan. She'd picked up two thick books at the local indie bookstore to read while doing nothing but soaking up the warm sun and drinking exotic, fruity drinks with umbrellas. Kelly took her hair down, picked up her backpack, scrolled to her boarding pass, and set off for the gate to paradise.

She stowed her carry-on under the seat in front of her as her fellow passengers jockeyed for the overhead storage space. She always traveled light, typically checking one medium-sized bag and carrying a smaller one for her laptop, iPad, and snacks. She gave her drink order to the attentive flight attendant and wiped her seat belt, tray table, and the arm of her seat with the disinfectant wipe she pulled from the package.

"Do you have one of those to spare?" the woman across the aisle asked, pointing to the bright-yellow package in Kelly's hand. The woman was in her mid-sixties, with jet-black hair and penciled-on eyebrows. "That's a great idea," she said pointing to the package in Kelly's lap. "Don't want to get sick before we even get there."

Kelly handed her one of the damp wipes.

"Are you headed to Miami for business or pleasure?"

"Just a connection," Kelly said, hoping to end the conversation.

"Someplace fun and exotic?"

Before she had a chance to answer, the woman continued. "My husband and I are staying for a week in South Beach. He had a meeting he couldn't get out of. He's flying in tomorrow."

"Enjoy yourself," Kelly said, hoping she didn't sound too rude. The other passengers were starting to file in, and she didn't want to spend the entire flight talking with a stranger. She wanted to relax and enjoy the bestselling lesbian adventure book in her lap.

Kelly occasionally glanced up as dozens of people passed her row, chatting and looking ahead for their seat. Rollaway suitcases were pulled behind personal travelers, some in shorts, others in jeans. Briefcases stocked with laptops and paperwork hung over the shoulders of business travelers dressed in Brooks Brothers' suits or expensive classic dresses.

Two women obviously traveling together walked by, but not before one of them gave her more than a passing glance and a knowing nod. Jeez, did everyone cheat, Kelly asked herself. An overweight man in a rumpled suit stopped in the aisle and rudely tossed his briefcase onto the seat next to her. It took him two attempts to heave his carry-on into the bin above her. Every time Kelly flew, she was always afraid of a suitcase falling on her head and breaking her neck. If there ever was a time to worry about that, this man was it. Finally, he fell into the seat behind her.

She scrolled through her phone for any last-minute messages or crises from one of her foremen. Since she had an all-female workforce, forewomen was probably more accurate, but it was a pain in the ass to say. She wasn't hung up on labels. She trusted her crew, yet things did come up that needed her attention or approval to move forward. It was her company, and she shouldered all the responsibility.

Her parents had sent a note telling her to have a good time, and one of her brothers said to make him proud and fuck everybody who was willing. Joe could be such a crude ass sometimes, she thought. No. Strike that. All the time. But he was her favorite and only eleven months younger. One of her friends was still hinting she'd gladly take Suzanne's place, not in her bed, but in the upscale room at the resort. When Kelly had booked the trip, she had shared the link with her friends, who went gaga over photos of the rooms, grounds, and beautiful women. The trip had cost a small fortune, and Kelly had originally balked at the idea, but now, she was definitely ready for this trip.

She'd worked practically nonstop through high school to afford four years of college. Her scholarship was only for tuition, and she still had major expenses to cover on her way to a teaching career. She'd discovered her interest in electricity and shifted her focus. Unlike most of her friends at Logan High and those that had gone on to traditional college, Kelly had saved every penny, nickel, and dollar she earned, getting her union card with far less student-loan debt than her peers. She had made her last loan payment eighteen months after starting her first job and was thrilled to be out from under that albatross.

Kelly turned off her phone, pushed all negative thoughts aside, and opened her book, symbolically beginning her vacation.

CHAPTER THREE

The throng of passengers surged toward the gate attendant, jockeying for position to get in front of the person behind them and secure the coveted overhead storage space. Matt didn't understand why they didn't just pay the measly twenty-five dollars and check their luggage. It would certainly make for a smoother and quicker boarding.

When she was a member of the corporate life, she'd traveled several times a month, and flying had become nothing but a pain-in-the-ass hassle. After getting knocked in the head by a wayward backpack or oversize shoulder bag wielded by a rude or unsuspecting passenger heading down the aisle like they were the only one on board too many times, she always boarded last. When she flew first class it was worse, with everyone looking at her and her fellow passengers to see if they were someone famous.

Matt handed her boarding pass to the gate agent, who scanned it. When the green light lit up, she looked at her screen. "Have a good flight, Ms. Parker." Matt murmured her thanks and followed Becca and Sandra down the jetway.

An overweight, rude man, wearing a suit that might have fit him thirty pounds ago, jumped in front of Matt just as she was about to enter the aircraft. He was juggling a cup of Starbucks and a phone, dragging a carry-on that should have been checked. Becca and Sandra continued down the aisle to their seats. She exchanged a look of disbelief with a fifty-something flight attendant with dyed red hair and too-white teeth. The man stopped at the last row in first class, blocking her path as he struggled to get his bag into the overhead space. The flight attendant watched him, then looked at Matt. He was in first class, and she probably should have offered some assistance, but she turned her attention to passengers stacking up behind them instead. Matt couldn't blame her. The guy was an asshole.

Her gaze wandered and landed on the passenger in the sixth row. The morning sunlight streamed through the window onto her blond hair. From what little Matt could see, she was attractive and had a copy of the latest book of one of Matt's favorite lesbian authors in her lap. The woman had good literary taste, she thought. When Matt glanced up, the woman was looking at her. Matt's pulse skittered as the woman's green eyes met hers. An electric current passed through her. It was a familiar yet dormant sensation she hadn't been sure she'd ever experience again. Her breath hitched, and her mouth was suddenly very dry.

"That's a great book," she somehow managed to say. Her hands were sweating, and little butterflies were dueling in her stomach. Tingling was also going on farther south of the butterfly fight zone. A puzzled look crossed the woman's face.

"*Renegade.*" Matt pointed to the book in her lap. "I love Joanna Baines. She's a great writer." Matt had no idea she was going to say any of that and was shocked the words appeared to flow smoothly out of her mouth. She was so rattled by her instant attraction to the woman, she had a hard time remembering her own name.

Recognition flashed across the woman's face when she realized Matt must be a lesbian. Why else would she have read the lesbian romantic-intrigue novel? Like her short, spiky haircut and her tailored shirt and shorts weren't enough of a clue. The woman smiled, and two dimples appeared in her cheeks. Matt's pulse skittered a little more.

"Don't tell me how it ends," she said, her eyes sparkling.

She had a soft Southern drawl, and Matt immediately thought of honey on a hot summer day. A tickle ran down Matt's spine. "My lips are sealed." She used her thumb and finger to mimic locking them with a key.

The woman's eyes shot to her lips, and from this angle, Matt saw a spark. The butterflies in her stomach swarmed.

Matt wanted to say more, but the man chose that moment to flop into his seat, and Matt had no choice but to continue down the aisle.

"Enjoy" was all she was able to say, but their lingering eye contact said much more.

Her shaky legs carried her to her aisle seat next to Sandra. She pulled out her iPad, then stowed her bag beneath the seat in front of her.

"What took you so long?" Becca asked from her seat next to the window.

"She was making time with the blonde in first class," Sandra said.

Matt's head turned. "What?"

"The woman, in first class," Sandra repeated. "I saw you talking to her."

"What? What did I miss?" Becca careened her neck over the seat in an obvious attempt to see who Sandra was talking about.

"Give it up, Bec. You'll never see her from where you are," Sandra said, pulling Becca back into her seat.

"I was just making conversation while that guy was hogging the entire aisle like he owned it," Matt said, hoping she didn't sound as rattled as she felt.

"I don't know," Sandra said in a conspiratorial tone. "Your face lit up like you saw presents under the Christmas tree."

"And what am I going to do about it?" Matt said, then realized she'd just admitted to the attraction. The best defense is a strong offense was the theory, anyway. "I don't even know her name, and we *are* in an airplane, for God's sake."

"Ever heard of the mile-high club?" Sandra nudged her with her shoulder.

"Ew," Becca said. "An airplane bathroom? How romantic," she added sarcastically.

"Romance has nothing to do with it." Sandra winked at Matt. "There's something to be said about anonymity. You never have to worry about the awkward morning after, and you can really cut loose."

Matt was spared any more conversation about sex and airplanes as the recorded pre-flight announcements began.

An hour into the flight, she was still thinking about the woman in 6B when she saw her step into the aisle and head for the lavatory. If she were honest with herself, Matt would have admitted she'd thought of nothing else since she'd sat down. She saw attractive women every day, and more than a few flirted with her, but what was it about this one that had caught and held her attention? She wasn't pretty. She was gorgeous. Her dimples added to her beautiful face, and her hair looked thick enough to glide through her fingers. Matt didn't believe in love at first sight and knew her pheromones had been sorely neglected, but was it something else? She wrote about instant chemistry, and her books flew off the shelves, so there must be something to the concept. When she'd met Andrea she'd felt a jolt of attraction, but nothing like the earth-moving thunderbolt she'd experienced an hour ago. With all the talk about sex on her vacation, her mind had to be playing tricks on her body. Yes, that must be it.

Just before she opened the door, the woman turned and looked directly at her.

Matt's row was only a few behind the first-class section, and even from this distance she couldn't miss the expression of interest and maybe even invitation in the woman's eyes. Even if she were up for it, a quickie with a lover would be exciting, but it seemed downright crude otherwise. Even if it was the first-class bathroom, a toilet was a toilet anywhere. However, when 6B turned and looked at her before she closed the lavatory door behind her, Matt almost changed her mind.

Chapter Four

Y ou were right," Kelly said to the woman who had commented on the book she was about to read. They were the only two at the checkout counter of a small kiosk. When the woman turned, Kelly was looking directly into the bluest eyes she'd ever seen.

She'd intentionally taken her time departing the aircraft, hoping to run into the woman again. After their brief conversation when she'd boarded, Kelly had turned in her seat and watched the woman walk down the aisle. When the woman sat down, their eyes met again. Kelly's pulse rate had rocketed, and she hadn't minded getting caught looking.

The woman was in her mid-thirties and several inches taller than Kelly. Her dark hair and blue eyes were an unusual combination, and she wrenched her brain back to high school biology to remember if that was even possible. It didn't matter. The woman was captivating. She was wearing a pair of shorts that showed long, tan legs, a long-sleeve shirt, and well-worn deck shoes. The bag over her shoulder was expensive but well used, her perfume light and alluring.

When Kelly had seen her, the first thing she'd thought of was the phrase that the best way to get over someone is to keep your mind occupied and focus on something else. Her "something else" that had kept her mind busy was imagining the way the woman's lips would feel trailing a fire down her skin, how her desire would increase and match the rapid cadence of her heart. How it would feel to have hands roam freely over her soft, smooth skin. The sight of an erect nipple, the first touch of the woman's warm, wet center, the taste of desire. Kelly didn't need to get over Suzanne. She was old news. They'd planned this trip months ago, and it had been shortly after everything was paid for when she told Suzanne to get lost.

"The book. It was just as good as you said it would be. However, I only got through chapter two. My mind kept drifting to other things," she replied, maintaining the direct eye contact only lesbians knew. The woman returned it.

"Hopefully something pleasant."

"Yes, it was," Kelly said, hoping it was clear she was thinking about her. "Is someone meeting you?" Kelly asked, pointing to the sign in the distance indicating baggage claim was straight ahead.

"No. Just a connection. You?"

"Not anymore," Kelly said without thinking. Suzanne was supposed to meet her here after attending her sister's wedding, but she barely wondered if they'd run into each other.

"Is that good or bad?"

"Doesn't matter anymore. Do you have time for a drink?" Kelly asked, uncharacteristically stepping out on a limb. By the surprised look on the woman's face, she was sorry she had.

The woman frowned, three vertical lines appearing between her perfectly arched eyebrows. She hesitated as if she wanted to say more. Was she weighing her options? Should she have a drink, maybe something more, and catch a later flight? Pass over a quickie in a private room in the executive lounge?

"I'd love to but—"

"No worries," Kelly said before the embarrassment of being shot down hit her. "I understand. Have a good rest of the day."

"You too," the woman replied, and Kelly watched her walk away. She was several yards away when she turned and looked over her shoulder. Their eyes met, and a buzz of pleasure shot through her.

"WTF, Kelly?" she said, popping her AirPods into her ears. She loved the invention that allowed her to talk to herself without looking like a weirdo. "You drool all over the woman in your mind, and you're so out of practice you can't even close the deal. Goddamn Suzanne. What a complete waste of time."

She stopped at the bank of monitors to locate her connecting gate. She needed to take the train to gate D32 but decided to check her messages first. Her phone had blown up when she'd turned it back on shortly after landing. She had plenty of time.

The first message was a robo-call offering to buy her house for cash in seven days. The second, third, fourth, and fifth were from Suzanne—again. She'd stopped listening to her messages after hearing Suzanne try to explain her way out of what had been blatantly obvious. At first, it had been quite comical, but after dozens more, she was done. She hit the delete button. It didn't matter how good in bed she was. Kelly's self-respect was worth more. She erased the rest of her messages without listening to them. She needed to block her calls but just hadn't taken the time to figure out how to do it.

Kelly was distracted handling a last-minute crisis at work, and she missed the first train to get her to the terminal that held her gate, the door on the next one smacking her in the shoulder as she hustled inside. A soft, yet official-sounding voice fussed at her to use caution when entering or leaving the train. A lady with three kids shook her head disapprovingly at her.

Kelly continued her lateness getting to her gate. First, she took a wrong turn, then had to make a detour due to new flooring being installed. She made it to the gate just as the last boarding announcement was made and hustled into her seat without looking around.

CHAPTER FIVE

"Welcome to the Palms Resort and Spa, ladies." A tall, thin woman in tan pants and a pale-blue short-sleeve shirt with a white mandarin collar greeted them as they stepped into the hotel lobby. It was after nine, local time.

"Thank you, Carol," Sandra replied, reading her name badge. "We have a reservation under the name Howser."

"Is this your first time on the island?"

"Yes, it is." Becca answered.

Matt let Becca and Sandra take care of the check-in details as she looked around. A typical Caribbean island resort, the spacious lobby had no doors, the entrance a large archway held up by two huge columns. A porte cochere allowed for luggage and guests to be out of the direct sun or rain as they entered or departed. The floors were eighteen-inch tile set in a diamond pattern. Everything was decorated in cool tones.

"If you'd like to have a seat, I'll get your paperwork." Carol pointed to a comfortable-looking couch to her left, not the chairs in front of a large desk.

"A refreshment?" a woman dressed similarly to Carol asked as she approached. She held up a tray with three glasses of green liquid floating in ice, a cucumber slice on the rim. In her other hand was a pair of tongs, with which she held out a white washcloth that was surprisingly cold. "To freshen up from your flight," she added before walking away.

The towel was a welcome relief to the grime of all-day travel and the humidity that had hit her when she stepped off the plane. The airport didn't have a jetway, and they'd exited directly down a set of stairs onto the tarmac. Matt wiped her hands, arms, face, and the back of her neck. How refreshing.

"If you will follow me, ladies, I'll give you a quick tour of the grounds. We do all your check-in paperwork in your room. Your luggage will follow shortly."

Matt followed Becca and Sandra as Carol showed them around, pointing out the spa, (maybe), gym, (definitely not), the pool, (another maybe), and the path to the beach, (a definite yes). The lighting was subdued, with just enough to see but not too much to ruin the resort's peaceful evening ambiance.

After they finished the paperwork, their luggage arrived, and Carol left them with information on the breakfast buffet and the taxi service on the island.

"You get the big room," Becca said. "We'll take these two." She pointed to two open doors on the other side of the large seating area.

"Why does she get the big room?" Sandra asked, in a joking tone.

"Because it's her trip," Becca said, as if the real answer was *Duh*. "You don't expect her to entertain in a dinky room that shares a bathroom, do you?"

"But you expect me to?"

"I've seen you naked, Sandra. Get over it."

Matt shook her head at her friends' playful banter as she wheeled her suitcase into her room.

Becca was right; this was a very nice room. It was almost larger than her bedroom at home. Several pillows adorned a king-sized bed that was centered under an oscillating ceiling fan. A small sitting area next to a patio door featured an overstuffed chair and small couch. The bath was to her left, and, in addition to a two-person jet tub, it had a large walk-in shower and double-sink vanity.

It was late, but their bodies were still on West Coast time, three hours behind the blue numbers on the clock on the nightstand.

Becca shouted from the common area. "Grab a cocktail from the minibar, Mattie." Becca's voice was muffled from the thick carpet in Matt's room. "We're going out on the patio."

Large shrubs offered a level of privacy Matt appreciated, since their rooms were on the third floor. The air was thick with humidity, and the slight breeze caused goose bumps on her arms. They sat in comfortable rattan chairs, a table where they could eat breakfast in front of them.

"So, now that we're here, do you have any other surprises for me?"

"Nope," Becca replied. "No plans other than sun, sand, and sex."

"And not necessarily in that order," Sandra added, her eyebrows bouncing up and down.

"Jesus, Sandra. You're such a horn dog. Are you still nineteen?" Matt asked, banishing the image of 6B hovering above her.

"Not hardly," Sandra said dismissively. "But this *is* a lesbian resort, which means that lesbians are here. A *lot* of lesbians. I am in my element and am about to embark on two weeks that I plan to never forget."

"This looks like the kind of place where lovers come, not a singles' resort. Not that I'd actually know what a lesbian resort looks like," Matt added.

"We're here and we're single," Sandra said. "Other single women are bound to be here too. We'll just have to look for them. Don't want to miss an opportunity because we think two women are together when they're actually friends. Ditto for me, so don't sit or walk too close to me when we're in public," she said in a teasing tone.

Sandra and Becca carried most of the conversation, Matt's thoughts drifting to the last time she'd had sex. It had been the morning Andrea was due to leave. They'd both cried afterward. It wasn't as though Matt was afraid that she'd always think of Andrea when making love to someone else. It was simply that she'd been so occupied with raising Jordan and starting her new career, her sex drive had simply gone dormant and drifted away. Until she saw the woman in 6B. She had jump-started Matt's libido, and it was firing on all cylinders as she thought of her.

What would she do if, or more likely when, she realized she wanted to take her attraction to someone to the next level. Her flirting skills had definitely been in hibernation for years and would be more than a little rusty. She had, however, been able to make conversation with 6B. A flicker of hope danced in her stomach.

Becca laughed, and Matt pretended she'd been a part of the conversation all along. They chatted about a few more things, and forty-five minutes later, Becca and Sandra headed for their rooms. Taking another sip of her drink, Matt let her mind drift back to the day six years ago that had changed her life forever.

"Shit, shit, shit." Matt cursed under her breath as she hustled down the hall. The knock on the front door came just as she had successfully crept out of Jordan's bedroom. Those who had ever tried to get a rambunctious, inquisitive three-year-old down for a nap knew what she was talking about. She hurried to the door before the knocking woke her sleeping son. If whoever was on the other side interrupted his much-needed nap, that person would remember this day for the rest of their life. She didn't look through the peephole, intent on cutting off another round of knocking or, God forbid, the doorbell.

She flung open the door, ready to crucify the poor sap on the porch, and froze. The earth stopped turning. Birds fluttering in the trees stilled. Dark clouds slid over the sun on the warm September day. Mattingly Parker's life, as she had known it for the last eight years, was over. Standing before her were two men and one woman in formal army uniforms, a somber expression on their faces. This was the day she'd expected yet prayed would never come.

"Mattingly Parker?" the shorter of the two men asked.

Matt swallowed a gasp and forced her heart back down her throat, then opened the door to allow the three to step inside. Her carefully crafted world crumbled as they crossed the threshold of the house she and Andrea had bought five years ago and painfully remodeled.

The next hour passed in slow motion, each second ticking off like the bomb that had killed her wife. After they left, Matt closed the door and retraced her steps back down the hall where their son was unaware that his mother, the woman who gave him life, had died in the middle of the street in some godforsaken place only a few people could find on a map and even fewer cared about.

With a practiced hand, Matt lifted her son into her arms, careful not to wake him. She needed time to get her head around what her life would be like now that the death-notification team had climbed into their black government sedan and driven down their quiet street.

Matt remembered studying the five stages of grief in her psychology class years ago. She couldn't deny that Andrea, her wife of eight years, was dead. The three that had just left were evidence of that fact. Anger, bargaining, depression, and finally acceptance rounded out the stages that were anything but sequential stops on a line. She faced no allotted, prescribed time during which she waited out one phase and then moved on to the next. Grief came in waves, often when it was least expected. Matt was certain she wouldn't be immune to any of it. The fact that she now had the job of raising their son alone didn't matter. That the painters were coming next week or that the pool filter needed to be overhauled ceased to matter. That she was supposed to take Andrea's dress uniform to the cleaners was of little consequence. Neither the dozens of phone calls she had to make nor the throngs of well-meaning well-wishers stopped what Matt knew was inevitable—agonizing, excruciating, unbearable pain. But right now, at this moment, she needed to hold their child, the son Andrea had worked so hard to have, enduring months of fertility treatments, failed in-vitro procedures before finally giving birth to the dark-haired, blue-eyed boy who was the mirror image of his mother at this age.

Matt needed to smell his toddler scent, which today was a mixture of peanut butter and traces of their dog Pluto, and hold his lanky body that would someday grow into that of a man Andrea would be proud of. She needed this time alone with her son and her memories of Andrea.

Four months ago had been the obligatory good-bye party with their combined friends and family, barbecue burgers for the kids, and ribs and chicken for the adults. Everyone had kissed Andrea and lingered over long hugs before leaving their backyard hours after the sun went down. They had gone to bed emotionally spent and almost too tired to make love, until Andrea reached for her. Their nights together were numbered before they were separated by honor, duty, and a world away from each other.

Their lovemaking was soft and sweet, Matt memorizing every moment. As the deployment date grew closer, their coupling grew more frantic, with quickies in the hall, on the couch, and in the tub, both of them knowing it could be the last time they shared their love for one another. They took walks, played with Jordan, and constantly touched each other, as if fearing their connection would be lost. The morning Andrea left was filled with tears and last-minute kisses as Matt watched the woman she loved walk through the security checkpoint, turn and wave one last time, and walk away.

Andrea was able to call once a week and, through the magic of video calls, was able to watch Jordan play or spit out his peas that he suddenly decided he didn't like. Matt would rather not see Andrea until she came home, the constant reminder of what she was missing too painful. But their calls weren't about her. They were about Andrea keeping a connection to the family she'd left behind in a world that, at times, made no sense. Jordan wouldn't remember her, but unbeknownst to Andrea, Matt had recorded every call. She never watched them but had kept them for just this reason: so Jordan would know Andrea's smile when she looked at him, hear her laugh at one of his silly antics, and see that the dimple in his right cheek was in the exact place as his mother's. Several times Jordan was asleep when Andrea was able to call, and Matt angled the camera toward him so Andrea could simply watch the rhythmic rise and fall of his chest while they spoke quietly.

Tears streamed down Matt's cheeks as she silently wept for the woman who had swept her off her feet eight years ago. The woman who had battled Matt's fears and showed her everyday just how much she loved her. Andrea was the third leg in their little family stool that, in an instant, threatened to topple over.

Matt paced back and forth across the small balcony, shaking off the sorrow that at one time had threatened to consume her. This was today, not six years ago when she had to force herself out of bed every morning. She had moved on, or at least she was trying to.

Matt heard Carol giving the same tour to another late-arriving guest, and she caught a glimpse of blond hair as she passed three flights below. Finishing her drink and determined to make the most of this vacation, Matt went inside, closing and locking the heavy sliding door behind her.

Chapter Six

"Shit." Matt tossed the covers aside and got out of bed. If she couldn't sleep, she might as well go down to the beach and watch the sun rise. She'd been restless most of the night, dreaming of a blond woman with dimples and a gorgeous smile. She pulled on a pair of shorts and a T-shirt and quietly opened her bedroom door. It was dark, and she used the light on her phone to make her way into the small kitchen. She prepared a pot of coffee, and as the water dripped into the pot, she retraced her steps back to her room to brush her teeth and find her flip-flops. By the time she grabbed a small bag for her room key and her phone, the coffee was ready. Even though Becca and Sandra wouldn't be up for hours, Matt left a note, and after filling a small, disposable to-go cup and snapping on the lid, she softly closed the suite door behind her.

The grounds of the resort were quiet as she strolled along the walkway. The sidewalk was wet in places from an errant sprinkler, and a worker was using a long-handled squeegee to remove the standing water. Matt was careful not to slip. The pool bar was locked, and rows of neatly lined deck chairs flanked the calm water. Several accent lights were on, giving the water a soothing, blue color. Palm trees stood tall, while others leaned away from the shore, the effect of relentless hurricane winds.

Matt slipped off her shoes before she stepped off the sidewalk. The sand was soft, and she hoped she didn't step on something she couldn't see in the early dawn. The last thing she wanted was to cut her foot on a broken shell or, worse, a piece of glass and not be able to get in the water for two weeks.

Three rows of beach chairs ran parallel to the shoreline, their adjacent umbrellas closed for the night. The sky was a pale shade of orange as the sun crept closer to making its morning debut. Matt tried to clear her mind as she walked on the hard sand packed by the incoming tide. She had never been good at simply enjoying peace and quiet or the beauty of nature. She had to be busy, whether it was writing, doing something with or for Jordan, or building something in her workshop. It wasn't as if she didn't like being alone. On the contrary, she enjoyed her solitary time, but she needed to be active. She often worried what she would do when she got too old to do the things she enjoyed. When her aging body wouldn't let her mow the yard, trim the bushes, or create something in her workshop, she'd go mad. She knew that someday the arthritis in her hands would make it impossible for her to type comfortably, so she'd been experimenting with a talk-to-text software a friend had recommended. It was hard to be creative and, at the same time, remember to add correct punctuation. Something about saying the words quote, period, comma, and end quote jarred her muse. No way could she do it when writing erotica. Talk about coitus interruptus, so to speak. She firmly believed in the adage about teaching old dogs new tricks. She thought about Jordan and then quickly chided herself that this trip was about her, and Jordan was in good hands.

The beach chairs and pattern on the umbrellas signaled a different hotel, and after four or five changes, Matt turned around and headed back in the direction she'd come. She settled into a chair just as the sun split the horizon.

The morning sky exploded in color, and the crystal-blue water sparkled. A sailboat drifting silently across the horizon caught her attention, and when she looked a little farther to her right, she spotted a woman sitting alone on the beach about a hundred yards away. She couldn't make out any specific details except that she was gazing into the sunrise, her long hair blowing in the soft breeze.

She reminded Matt of the woman on the plane in seat 6B, and her pulse kicked up a couple of beats. 6B had long hair and the cutest dimples when she smiled. She was sure the woman hated to be called cute because of them. She looked like she was a professional and wanted to be taken seriously.

The connection she had felt with 6B astonished her. She'd looked at hundreds of women since Andrea died, and never had she felt even the slightest spark. So what was it about 6B that caught and held her attention, even now?

The gentle crashing of the waves was soothing, and when she jerked awake, she realized she'd dozed off. Somewhere behind her, a rooster was crowing. It was a rooster, right? How in the hell would she know, since she was a city girl? Matt looked around and now saw others walking the same path she'd taken. Several couples, both lesbian and straight, held hands as they strolled along the water's edge. Two women with knock-out bodies ran by, and Matt had to admit they were just as attractive running away as they were running toward her. Matt looked more carefully, but the woman she wanted to be 6B was nowhere in sight. Her stomach growled, and she went to find something to eat.

Matt was enjoying her second cup of coffee as one of the many wait staff cleared away her breakfast plate. She'd been greeted warmly when she arrived thirty minutes ago, every worker smiling and saying good morning. The buffet choices were plentiful, with two kinds of potatoes, sausage, bacon, assorted fruit, Danish, bagels, and toast. A separate section contained slices of meat and cheese and tomatoes, while the table to the right prepared omelets to order. Tables of various sizes were scattered around the patio area, protected from the elements or the morning sun by large shade sails or thick canopies of trees. Two women were sitting beside her, never looking up from their phones. Two others, who Matt guessed were in their late sixties, sat next to them, yet they were engaged in conversation. What a difference a generation makes, she thought.

Matt's breath caught when 6B stopped at the hostess desk. She blinked several times, believing that her mind was playing tricks on her, but as the woman started walking toward her, she realized she hadn't made a mistake. She quickly turned away, not sure why she felt so unprepared to deal with her this morning. Their airport flirting had been harmless. But now she was here.

It appeared the woman was alone, but someone as attractive as she was wouldn't be at a lesbian resort by herself. When they met at the airport, hadn't she said she was no longer meeting someone? Maybe the other woman was still getting ready. Maybe she didn't eat breakfast. Maybe 6B had exhausted her last night, and she was still sleeping. *Jesus, Matt. Get a grip.* It was suddenly very warm, and she shifted in her chair, hoping not to be seen, yet watching 6B out of the corner of her eye

❖

The hostess checked Kelly off the guest list and led her to a small table out of the main traffic area.

"Coffee, ma'am?"

A short woman with wavy red hair and green eyes was standing in front of her holding a coffee carafe. Her name tag read Dorothy.

Kelly turned over her cup and placed it back in the saucer. "Yes. Thank you."

Dorothy gave Kelly the rundown on the buffet items as she poured the hot coffee into the cup. The smell was wonderful, and even though she'd made a small pot in her room, nothing beat the first cup over breakfast.

Kelly was tired but hoped a good breakfast and several gallons of coffee would kick-start her day. She'd arrived late to her room, where champagne, fresh fruit, and cheese were waiting. The top sheet on the large bed had been turned back, the lights low, the music soft. Very romantic. Two fluffy robes hung on silver hooks behind the bathroom door. The tub was big enough for two, maybe even three, and a sliding door for privacy separated it from a large shower with a waterfall nozzle on each end. The management had thought of everything a loving couple could ask for. Too bad it was all wasted on just her.

Even though she'd been exhausted when she arrived, Kelly hadn't been able to sleep and had finally given up and gone to seek the calm, peaceful water of the ocean.

She was a water girl, having grown up on the shores of southern California. Her mother said she'd learned how to surf almost before she learned how to walk. Her father loved to be in the water and would often take his only daughter out with him. Her older brothers would tag along, but she was definitely Daddy's girl and loved the time she spent with him. Whenever she had to think, she always came back to the water.

Kelly had thought about what went wrong in her relationship with Suzanne. They'd been happy, or at least she'd thought they were. Sure, after three years the overwhelming lust and passion had dimmed, but they had the same friends, similar tastes, and a compatible temperament. Was that it? Were they too much alike that they bored each other? Was there no challenge anymore? No yin or yang? She'd concluded that they'd just drifted apart, and she hadn't even realized it until it was over. At least they hadn't gotten married or co-mingled any finances. That would have been a nightmare. The worst was that she had lost a friend in the whole mess. Or someone she'd thought was her friend.

Two cups later she sauntered over to the buffet and filled her plate. She was starving and didn't feel guilty about grabbing a heaping spoon of scrambled eggs, five strips of bacon, and a cherry Danish. After all, breakfast was the most important meal of the day.

As she ate, Kelly glanced around. She felt like someone was watching her, but everyone was either talking to their table mates, eating, or minding their own business. The nagging feeling continued, but this was a lesbian resort. Maybe a woman was admiring the view. She chuckled at her own self-importance. Like, at thirty-seven, she was a prize catch.

Kelly finished her breakfast and looked around the small, outdoor café. Because of the large umbrellas to catch leaf or bird droppings from the many trees overhead, it felt like a tropical rain forest, without the rain. There were several open tables and no one waiting to be seated, so Kelly opened the island newspaper to the front page.

Her bladder signaled her that it was time to go, and she left a big tip on the table and gathered her things. She'd head for the water again, this time to get in and enjoy an early morning swim, followed by a nap in the warm sun.

CHAPTER SEVEN

Matt accepted two towels from the perky brunette womaning the towel bar. Her name tag read Charise, and she had to be at least six feet tall.

"I have not seen you here before. Is this your first time joining us?" Charise asked. Her teeth were pristine white, her eyes welcoming. Her accent was Jamaican.

"Yes, my first day," Matt answered. "I was out here this morning before the sun came up, and it was spectacular."

"Yes, our sunrises are beautiful and our sunsets romantic." She looked behind Matt before asking, "Are you here alone?"

"At the moment, yes, but not here at the resort." She shook her head. "My friends prefer to sleep the day away and miss all this beautiful sunshine."

"Ah," Charise replied. "Are you here with a lover?"

Matt was taken aback by her direct question. She'd never been asked if she was somewhere with a lover. I guess we Americans *are* hung up about sex, she thought.

"No, I'm not. Just a getaway with a few friends."

"Would you like for me to point you out to other single women?"

Again, Matt was surprised. Was Charise trying to pimp her out? She studied her for a moment before answering. "No, thank you."

"Would you like for me to point out other single women to you?"

Matt glanced around. Was she joking? By the expression on her face she was completely serious. "Thank you, Charise, but I'm just here with friends, and I think I can handle that part myself."

"Okay, but if you change your mind, please let me know."

Matt walked away like she'd just been shopping at a high-end boutique—or a meat market. She stepped onto the warm sand, eager to get away from Charise and her matchmaking.

Most of the beach chairs were already occupied, and she scanned the area for three that appeared to be vacant. She found only one, sandwiched between two others. One was occupied with the edge of a book peeking out from under a towel, the other an elderly woman wearing a large sun hat even though she was under an umbrella. When Becca and Sandra finally made their way down to the beach, they were on their own.

"Is this chair taken?" she asked to the woman to the right of the empty chair.

"No," she grunted, then turned over onto her stomach.

So much for conversation with her, Matt thought. She spread out her towels on the chair and put her water flask, sunscreen, and notebook on the table on the opposite side from the woman.

She scanned the beach and saw women of all shapes and sizes, some with glorious bodies they obviously worked hard for, and others who spent far too much time behind a desk or on the couch. Matt was somewhere in the middle. A couple with a toddler walked in front of her, their arms laden with towels, beach bags, and toys. That was her and Andrea many years ago, when they'd taken a trip to San Diego. Jordan had loved the water, making sandcastles and burying his mama in the sand. Her heart ached for a couple of beats.

Matt thought that the phrase time heals all wounds was partially right. The only thing time did was ease the debilitating effect of wounds that would never go away.

The first week after she lost Andrea had been a blur, when all she wanted to do was stay in bed and forget the world existed. She wanted to stop breathing so the unbearable pain would cease, and the gut-wrenching despair would end. But she couldn't. She had Jordan to think of and take care of. Her parents, Sandra, and Becca were taking turns, but Jordan was her responsibility, and he was the only thing that got her out of bed each morning.

How did others who lost a spouse move on to find someone else to love? Would she wake up one day and just know? Would she see a sign of some kind? Would she know it if there was? She'd put her personal life on hold for so long she didn't know if she'd recognize an opportunity if it arrived via FedEx, signature required.

Thirty minutes later, her watch chimed, a reminder to apply more sunscreen. She usually tanned pretty easily, but she didn't want to risk getting sunburned on the first day. The woman beside her was snoring softly, and the occupant of the chair on the other side hadn't yet returned. She thought it awfully rude for people to come down early, stake their claim on a chair, then return when they were ready. By the looks of the vacant chairs and the few people in the water, this was obviously a common practice on this beach. She'd written a dozen pages on her new book, and a few more were itching to get out and onto the page.

Another ding on her watch, and Matt put her notebook and pen into her bag. The woman was gone, the other chair still empty. More chairs were occupied, and a dozen kids were playing in the water.

With the exception that this was a lesbian resort, Jordan would love it here, she thought, as a jet ski motored far enough away to be almost soundless. Three people were on paddleboards, two parasailers floating in the clear-blue sky above a bright-orange jet boat. A couple to her right, if body language was any indication, was obviously arguing, while another was kissing almost to the point of being inappropriate. That scene, and the very busty redhead walking by watching them, were inspiring, and Matt penned a few thousand words for a new erotic short story, appropriately set in a lesbian resort. She was so engrossed in a torrid sex scene, she didn't notice another woman approaching. When she turned to say hello, the words froze on her lips. 6B was sitting down beside her.

Chapter Eight

Kelly had stalled long enough. She'd been in the water too long and noticed her skin getting pink. She'd been ready to get out a while ago when she noticed the woman from the plane in the chair right next to hers. Why was she hesitating? It wasn't like her to shy away from something uncomfortable or someone so beautiful. She'd sensed the attraction between them, and for crying out loud, she was single. She couldn't just go back to her room because her key was in her bag tucked under her chair. She wondered again about the woman's relationship status, as she was obviously on the beach alone.

Kelly managed to get to her chair and reach for her book before the woman noticed her. She couldn't see her eyes behind the dark, wraparound sunglasses, but she felt the woman's eyes glide over her before she broke into a dazzling smile.

"Do you come here often?" the woman asked, sliding her sunglasses down her nose. Her blue eyes were more vivid than the first time she saw them, the color of the cloudless sky overhead.

Kelly couldn't help but laugh. "Does that line usually work for you?"

"Actually, I'm a little out of practice," she admitted, blushing a little.

Kelly's antenna extended. "Is that because you're married?"

The woman didn't look away.

"No."

"Long-term girlfriend?"

"No."

"Are you going to tell me that you never need to make the first move? That attitude would be disappointing."

"No. That would make me a conceited asshole, wouldn't it?"

Kelly tilted her head and raised her eyebrows questioningly.

"Widow," the woman said.

"I'm sorry for your loss." Kelly had said that same phrase before to other people, and it sounded so trite, but what else was there? You had to say something.

"Thank you."

"I didn't mean to…"

The woman waved off Kelly's apology for her flippant bantering. But how could she have known?

"No worries. It's been a long time." She extended her hand. "Matt Parker."

Kelly wiped her damp palm on her towel before shaking hers. "Kelly Newsome."

"A much prettier name than 6B."

"6B?"

"Your seat on the flight from Atlanta to Miami."

"Oh yeah. Right," Kelly said. Warmth spread through her that Matt had remembered her. "And you were 'the woman on the plane.'" Kelly watched Matt's eyes light up like she suspected hers did.

"Just the woman?"

"If I tell you it was the really hot woman on the plane, will that make your head so big you'd block my sun? I came to get a tan."

Matt laughed, again a hearty laugh that made Kelly's stomach tingle.

"I'll try to keep control over myself." Matt's eyes skimmed over her body again. "And the tan you have looks great."

Kelly warmed all over, glad she'd gone ahead and bought a new red bikini and chosen to wear it today.

"At the risk of ending our interesting conversation, it appeared you were by yourself on the plane and you aren't saving a chair for anyone." Matt motioned. "Are you here alone?"

"Due to circumstances that will not ruin my day, it's just me," Kelly replied. "I'll pose the question right back at you."

"Did Charise try to hook you up with other singles?" Kelly laughed, and a pleasant tingle ran down Matt's spine.

"Yes, she did. I'm no prude, but I must admit that surprised me. I certainly didn't read about her services in the hotel brochure."

"Neither did I, but I guess they aim to make sure every guest has the time of her life."

"Maybe that's how they got their five-star rating."

"Have to give them credit for creative customer service."

"You didn't answer my question." Kelly was prodding her.

"My friends said I needed to get away, so they gave me this trip."

"Wow," Kelly said, squeezing some sunscreen into her palm. "Do they need any more friends? I'd dump mine in a heartbeat and go with yours." She watched Matt's eyes follow her hands as she spread lotion over her legs, and more than just her legs were heating up.

"You can probably ask them later. They're here with me. They were still asleep when I left this morning."

"Matt. That's an interesting name. Short for something?" Kelly asked, her voice a little raspy because she was trying to banish the image of Matt lazing in bed.

"Mattingly. Old family name. Lucky me," she replied sarcastically.

"Well, in the three minutes I've known you, I can say it suits you."

"I appreciate that, but it's caused me more confusion than any kid should have to endure."

Kelly thought for a moment, imagining boys and girls being separated by name. Matt was probably always in the wrong line. "I see your point," she said.

"I'm going to be nosy and ask why you're on a beautiful beach by yourself. If none of your friends wanted to come, you should dump them."

"I was bringing my girlfriend, but when she decided she'd rather fuck my best friend than be here with me, I rescinded my offer."

"Ouch," Matt said, grimacing.

"Surprisingly, I'm not broken up over it." Kelly had realized that was true shortly after discovering them. "I traded her ticket for one in first class, I already had the time off, and the room was paid for, so here I am, sitting next to the hot woman from the plane on my first day." She lay back in her chair, her legs outstretched, and caught Matt looking at her breasts again. She put her sunglasses on, but not before saying, "Don't run off."

Matt's heart skipped a beat or two. She was flirting. She hadn't done that in what felt like a lifetime ago. Actually, it *had* been a lifetime ago, her life with Andrea. She took another long look at Kelly. She had, what Sandra once called, curves in all the right places, and she wanted to trace them with her fingers, memorize them with her hands, and taste them with her tongue. And there was the same sizzle she'd felt when she saw her on the plane. Was that only yesterday? She suddenly felt a little light-headed.

Maybe what she was feeling was the vacation high. It was kind of like the fact that you spend money more easily when on vacation than you do at home. Was that it? Besides invigorating, what was she going to gain from this experience? Did she intend to mess the sheets with her? That thought excited and scared the hell out of her, even though that had been her intent on this trip. However, this opportunity with Kelly was very appealing. At home she was under the constant eye of either Andrea's parents, the Medal of Honor office, or Jordan. Each had their own agenda for her, and after six years she was weary of the personal invasion.

Matt knew Andrea's parents didn't care for her. They were polite but never went out of their way to make her feel welcome or part of their family. After Andrea was killed, they went so far as to actually buy the house across the street and move in. They were intrusive and tried to hide their over-vigilance under their inquiry about Jordan. She had often been questioned about a car in her driveway late at night, or was that a babysitter playing in the front yard with Jordan yesterday? In their minds, if Matt moved on with her life, she would be cheating on their daughter. They'd made that very clear more than a few times.

The Medal of Honor office was using Andrea's death to prove how progressive they were by awarding the medal to an openly out lesbian. The ceremony was weeks away, yet she received a call or email from them almost daily. They'd been subtle in their conversations with Matt and never went so far as to say she shouldn't date again, but their message was also very clear. They expected her behavior to equal the brave sacrifice of her wife. What did they think she was going to do? Post a video on Facebook of the widow of a Medal of Honor woman fucking some other woman during an orgy?

And then there was Jordan. Their nine-year-old son had his mother on a pedestal so high no one could get anywhere near the shrine he'd built to her. Last year when Matt had approached Jordan with the idea that she might start dating again, he was almost hysterical. He cried and screamed at her that she was forgetting about his mom and begged her not to. It was an awful scene and had shaken Matt more than she realized.

How do you explain that life goes on to a child who had lost the mother he idolized and had died a national hero? When she agreed to let Jordan attend camp, she knew her in-laws believed she was doing it to get him out of the house so she could carry on with her depraved lifestyle, as her mother-in-law Cynthia considered it. They'd had an ugly fight about it, but they quieted down when Jordan had convinced them it was his idea. So here she was for the next two weeks, where no one knew her and she didn't need to keep up appearances. She would be crazy to pass up this opportunity. And she wasn't crazy. At least not yet.

Kelly's phone ringing interrupted any further conversation. She glanced at it and swore.

"Work?" Matt asked.

Kelly frowned. "Ex."

"Girlfriend or best friend?"

"Best friend," Kelly replied, hitting the bright-red hang-up icon. She turned off the ringer and put her phone facedown on the table between them. "Right now, it's neck and neck as to who's left the longest voice mail."

"Have you spoken to either one of them?" Matt asked, not sure why, but curious, nonetheless.

"No. I have nothing to say to them now, or ever. But the gist of their long, expansive messages is basically that it's not what it looked like." Kelly turned and faced Matt. "Can I ask you something?"

"Sure," Matt answered, curious where Kelly would take the conversation but, surprisingly, eager to go anywhere with her.

"If you walked into *your* bedroom and saw *your* best friend fucking *your* girlfriend with a strap-on, what would you think it was?"

Matt choked on her mouthful of water. She sat up and coughed several times.

"Are you all right?" Kelly asked, taking off her sunglasses and looking her way.

Matt couldn't talk but nodded. Finally, she said, "Yes. I'm fine. Just went down the wrong way." She coughed a few more times. Kelly was waiting for her answer.

"Not much room for interpretation in that case."

Matt regained her breath and tried to keep her eyes on Kelly's, but the lure of cleavage at the top of Kelly's bikini top was too tempting. Matt's gaze dropped for just a second, and when it returned, the knowing look on Kelly's face made Matt blush.

"Thank you," Kelly said. "Any girl in my situation likes to know she's still attractive."

Matt's heart rate spiked. "That's definitely not a problem."

"Obviously Suzanne didn't think so."

"Obviously Suzanne is an idiot," Matt said. "Other than what you must have gone through, I'm glad you're here."

Kelly studied her for so long, Matt started to get nervous.

"Shit. I'm sorry. Here you are, a woman who'd been planning a romantic getaway with her girlfriend and recently found out said girlfriend was cheating on her with her best friend, and I'm hitting on you. That's not cool," Matt said apologetically. Kelly smiled, and Matt's heart skipped again.

"Actually," Kelly said, just before sliding her sunglasses back up her nose and settling back in her chair. "It is."

CHAPTER NINE

W ait," Becca said, grabbing Sandra's arm.

"What?"

"Look." Becca pointed toward the rows of white beach chairs. "First row from the water, about ten over. Under the green umbrella."

"Don't point." She slapped Becca's arm down.

"Hey, that hurt. They can't see me. They're not even facing this way," Becca said.

"Who?" Sandra asked, still not seeing whoever Becca was referring to.

"Mattie."

"Jeez, Bec. They're all green umbrellas. How am I supposed to find her?" Just then Sandra saw her. A woman in a red bikini was leaning in, saying something that made Matt laugh.

"For someone who didn't want to go on this trip, she sure isn't wasting any time," Becca said, almost in awe. "Good girl."

"Maybe they're just talking."

"Yeah, right. Like you were just talking to the little cutie in the itty-bitty yellow bikini a few minutes ago."

Becca and Sandra watched Matt and the woman for a few minutes before Becca said, "I'm not going to stand here all day while Mattie makes time with Miss Red Bikini. I'm going in the water. We can spy on them better from there." Becca kicked off her flip-flops and dropped her towel on top of them.

The water was cool, but not so cold it was unpleasant, and Sandra quickly caught up with her. "Let's swim out to that buoy." This time she pointed to a round yellow ball about thirty yards offshore. "We can hang onto that and watch from there."

"What do you think they're talking about?" Sandra asked, a little out of breath from the swim to the buoy.

"Hopefully not the weather," Becca replied.

"If Mattie doesn't make a move on her, I will."

"This trip isn't about you." Becca enjoyed teasing her.

"The hell it isn't. This island is crawling with lesbians. If that part isn't about me, nothing is."

Sandra wasn't a player, but she didn't spend too many nights alone if she didn't want to. Becca had always admired Sandra's viewpoint that sex was no more or less complicated than fulfilling any other natural bodily need. She, on the other hand, didn't need happily-ever-after before she got naked, but she did need to know a little more than just a name.

"Mattie looks tired," Sandra commented seriously.

"You would too if you had the same shit going on in your life that she does. I don't know how she deals with Harrison and Cynthia," Becca said, referring to Matt's in-laws. "They have their noses so far up into Mattie's life she can barely breathe. Did you hear the latest?"

"No, but I can only imagine. If they were my in-laws, I'd have told them to go fuck themselves a long time ago."

"It's not that easy," Becca said. "She wants Jordan to know his grandparents. It's what Andrea wanted."

"Not if she could see them now," Sandra commented. "Anyway, what did they do?"

Becca told Sandra the latest round of meddling Andrea's parents had inflicted on Matt. Andrea had been their only child, and when she died, they had literally erected a shrine on a large table in their home, complete with burning candles. As far as Becca knew, it was still there.

"Like I said..." Sandra held up her hand to stop Becca's comment. "I know, I know. It's not that easy."

"And it's none of our business," Becca added.

"Yes, it is." Sandra was still watching Matt and the woman. "We're her best friends, and we need to poke and prod her until she does what's good for her. We've always had to do that."

"But not in something like this. This is her life, and we need to be careful with what we say, or she'll think we're just as bad as they are."

Sandra frowned and shook her head. "No one will ever be that bad."

"Harrison is pressuring her to go on that speaking tour."

The Medal of Honor committee was trying to convince Matt to join several medal winners on a cross-country speaking tour to, in their words, "showcase the heroic actions of our armed forces."

"She isn't going to, is she?" Sandra asked. "It's nothing but a recruiting tour to sign up more strapping young men and women to eagerly go to places we don't belong and fight for something that's none of our business."

"Your personal politics aside, I don't think she'll do it." Becca and Sandra often disagreed about our military's role in world affairs, but their differences never infringed on their friendship.

"They're doing it to show they're not still a bunch of homophobes." Sandra continued. "I know how proud Mattie was of what Andrea was doing, but they'll parade her and Andrea's memory around for their own agenda. Jesus, she lost her wife, for God's sake, and they want her to relive it every day in front of a bunch of strangers?"

"She told me she hated Andrea for a long time after she was killed."

"What! You never told me that!" Sandra let go of the buoy and got a mouthful of water. She came up sputtering.

"She told me only a few weeks ago. I haven't had the chance to talk to you about it."

"What did she say?" Sandra coughed a few more times, clearing her lungs.

"She was having a hard time with Jordan and Harrison and Cynthia, and out of the blue she said she hated that Andrea loved the army more than her family. How she chose to re-enlist over staying home with her and Jordan. Andrea knew she'd be deployed again, putting her life in danger, and she did it anyway."

"I thought the same thing but kept my mouth shut."

"That was a first," Becca said. "You never keep your opinion to yourself."

"I know it's shocking. But somehow I managed."

"She was angry for a long time."

"Do you think she still is?" Sandra asked.

"No. I think that's passed."

"She's getting up," Sandra said, nodding in the direction of Matt and the woman. "Looks like she might be going to the bar." The woman was walking away but had left her towel and beach bag on her chair.

"Quick. Let's get over there and find out what's going on."

CHAPTER TEN

Matt watched Kelly walk away. She was just as attractive from this direction as she was sitting beside her.

"Keeping yourself entertained?" Sandra asked.

"Don't act like you don't know what we're talking about," Becca added.

"Jeez, ladies, pounce much?" Matt asked, her attention yanked away from watching Kelly walk across the sand. She hadn't seen her friends in the water, but it was obvious that's where they'd come from.

"Were you spying on me?"

"No. We were watching. Spying implies something clandestine, and we were anything but. Now spill," Becca said, sitting on the edge of Matt's chair.

"Where were you?"

"Doesn't matter. Spill." Becca waved her hands for emphasis.

"Her name is Kelly."

"Is she here with anyone?"

"No. She's by herself."

"A knockout like that does not come to a place like this alone. What's wrong with her?"

"Jesus, Sandra. Sometimes you're a real pig," Matt said. "There's nothing wrong with her. She caught her girlfriend with her best friend and traded her ticket for a first-class trip."

"Ouch." Becca grimaced. "Some girlfriend."

"Some friend," Sandra added.

"So, what have you two been talking about? Are you going to have lunch together? Dinner? Maybe a sleepover?" Becca asked, interrogating Matt.

"Jeez, Becca," Matt protested, putting her hand up to ward off Becca's barrage of questions. "We just met."

"And your point is?" Sandra added.

Matt looked at both her best friends and shook her head. They meant well. They could be a bit intense individually, but together they were overwhelming.

"We just met," Matt said again, as if that was her answer to their past, current and future questions. "The topic of a meal hasn't come up, and *if* it does, I think I can handle it."

"She's hot," Sandra said, as if Matt hadn't noticed. "If you don't move on her, Mattie, I will."

"Jesus, Sandra. Do you think you could be a little louder? I doubt if the group of twenty-year-olds down the beach heard you," Matt said, glaring at her. "I'm surprised to see you. Aren't you supposed to be chatting up some sweet thing at the bar?" Matt hoped she could deflect the conversation away from her and Kelly.

"Don't take that tone with me," Sandra said in mock anger. "I get laid pretty regularly, and don't you change the subject."

"I am not the subject."

"Oh yes, you are," Sandra added firmly, in her district-attorney voice. "This is just what you need. No-strings sex, out from under the prying eyes of your in-laws and Jordan's disapproval. This place is crawling with lesbians. You might not get another opportunity."

"You're contradicting yourself. If this place is crawling with lesbians, how could I not have an opportunity?"

"I mean with Kelly," Sandra said. "Every woman that walks by is checking her out. You're going to lose your chance."

When Matt hesitated, Becca said, "What are you afraid of, Mattie?"

"What are you talking about?" Matt knew exactly what Becca meant but needed a minute to figure out what to say.

"I mean, what are you afraid of?" Becca repeated her question, putting space between each word. "Don't overanalyze this. It's not like you're interviewing her to be Jordan's stepmother. It doesn't have to mean anything. Christ, you probably don't even know where she lives. She's perfect."

"I'm not afraid of anything." Even to her own ears she sounded lame.

"Bullshit." Becca always called it the way she saw it, and Matt knew it.

"Hi."

Matt jumped. She hadn't seen Kelly approach until she was almost right in front of her.

Matt prayed Sandra didn't say what she was obviously thinking. Sandra was polished and sophisticated, but when it came to her friends, she could be a loose cannon. Sandra looked at Matt, clearly waiting for an introduction.

"Kelly, these are my friends Becca Tresome and Sandra Howser."

"The 'best friends that brought you on this trip' friends?" Kelly asked, removing her sunglasses and shaking Sandra's outstretched hand. The movement caused her top to gap, exposing more flesh for Matt to gawk at.

"Yep, that's us," Sandra replied.

"Can I be your best friend too?" Kelly asked jokingly. "Matt told me what you did for her."

"It was nothing." Sandra shrugged. "And I'm tempted to say no, because I don't want to be your *friend*, but I may be a bit late."

Matt flushed with embarrassment at Sandra's blatant flirting. She wanted to walk into the blue water and keep walking, but that would allow Sandra to be alone with Kelly. Who knew what she'd say next?

"Come on, Sandra," Becca said, standing. "Let's go for a swim."

"We just got out," Sandra said, not taking her eyes off Kelly.

"Well, we're going back in," Becca said, tugging Sandra to her feet.

"I hope you get caught in a rip tide," Matt said, joking, as Becca pulled Sandra back toward the water. Sandra flipped her the bird.

"I like her," Kelly said.

"The Morris County judicial system hates her," Matt replied. "She's the founding partner of the most successful lesbian law firm in the city. You wouldn't know it, but she's very buttoned up nine to five."

"Very charming too."

A surge of jealousy trailed down Matt's spine. It would be just her luck that a woman she was finally interested in would want to be with Sandra instead.

"But she's not my type," Kelly added, as if she could read Matt's mind.

"With as much action as Sandra gets, she's everybody's type."

Kelly laughed. "Lucky girl. What's *your* type?" Kelly asked a few seconds later.

Matt's mind went blank. What was her type? It had been so long she wasn't sure she remembered. "I'm not sure."

"You're not sure?" Kelly asked.

"Well, it's been a while, and, as I said, I'm a little out of practice." And more than a little embarrassed to admit it, she thought.

"I'm sure it's like riding a bike. It'll come right back to you as soon as you hop on."

The thought of hopping on Kelly and riding her was very vividly playing in her head.

"My friends are harmless. They mean well. Don't take them seriously."

"I'm on vacation. I don't think seriously when I'm in a bikini." She winked at Matt.

"Funny," Matt said, letting her eyes dance over Kelly's bare skin. "I can't think seriously when you're in a bikini either."

Kelly gave her a long, appraising look, and more than a little heat spread through Matt and settled between her legs.

"Good, because I'm not into serious. I just want to relax and enjoy myself."

"Becca and Sandra said I needed to get laid."

Kelly slowly turned her head and stared at Matt, amusement and a bit of something else in her eyes.

"Jesus, the heat must be getting to me already. I can't believe I just said that." Matt dropped her head into her hands, mortified, her face hot with embarrassment. Whatever had possessed her? It was true, yes, but it wasn't something you typically spewed out of your mouth right after meeting someone. God, she was pathetic. Maybe she should just go back to the room, crawl back under the covers, and start the day over again. Maybe she'd wait till tomorrow.

"I don't sleep with someone within," Kelly glanced at the clock on her phone, then dropped it into her bag, "within forty-nine minutes of meeting them."

The sizzling look Kelly was giving her made Matt flush all over with another kind of heat.

"But I'm thinking with you, I might make an exception."

Matt wasn't sure she was able to speak. She didn't know what to say. *Okay? Thanks? Let's go to your room because I have two nosy roomies?* Kelly studied her, and Matt knew she had to say something, anything to keep this conversation going. Kelly had lobbed her interest out there, and unless Matt said something, it would crash and burn.

"I…uh…need to cool off," Matt said before thinking. She needed to get away from Kelly's direct, straightforward proposal before she embarrassed herself in front of this beautiful woman.

"I'll be right here when you get back," Kelly said as Matt forced herself not to run full speed into the cool water.

❖

Kelly enjoyed watching Matt walk the twenty yards to the water. She was wearing a pair of loose swim shorts and a bikini top, not the traditional tankini or sports bra most of the other women on the beach had on. Women in sports bras did nothing for her. It wasn't that she wasn't into sports or athleticism. On the contrary, she played lacrosse every Saturday in a mixed league. It was a great way to unwind and clear her head from the challenges of her week.

She preferred women in beachwear that was attractive as well as functional. And Matt was definitely attractive.

Her legs were firm, the muscles in her calves accentuated by the effort it took to get through the thick sand. She had great posture and moved gracefully across it. It wasn't just her obvious physical attraction to Matt that caused her to want to spend much more time with her inside than outside. It certainly wasn't rebound sex. She wasn't bouncing from Suzanne to Matt. She was long over her. It was Matt's rusty charm that had caught and held her attention. There was much more to Matt Parker, and Kelly wanted to know every inch of it.

CHAPTER ELEVEN

C an I get you ladies something for lunch?"
Kelly looked up from her book to see a tall, gorgeous woman in the hotel uniform of shorts and a pale-blue tank top standing in front of her. Her name tag said Doreen, and she was holding a menu in her outstretched hand.

Her stomach growled. She turned to Matt and asked, "Would you like to have lunch with me?"

"I thought you'd never ask," Matt teased her, taking a menu from Doreen.

"I'll give you a few minutes to decide. Can I freshen your drinks?"

"Absolutely," Kelly said, handing Doreen her empty tumbler. "I'm on vacation."

"Same as last time?" Doreen asked. This was Doreen's third time refilling her drink.

"I like the way you think," Matt said, nodding her agreement for another.

"What do you recommend?" Kelly asked Doreen, referring to the menu.

"The pizza is great, and any of our bar food is delicious. The wings are kind of messy though. I'll be right back with your drinks."

They decided to split a pizza, and when Doreen was out of earshot Kelly asked, "Is everyone on this island drop-dead gorgeous?"

"Must be a requirement to be hired here," Matt commented.

Kelly glanced around. "What happened to Sandra and...I'm sorry. I forgot. What was your other friend's name?"

"Becca." Matt looked at the women in the chairs surrounding them, then out toward the water. "I have no idea. They're around here somewhere. Sandra's undoubtably making time with some beauty, and Becca most likely has her nose in a legal brief."

Matt's statement contained no judgment, just facts. "It sounds like Becca needs to take some lessons from Sandra."

"Trust me. Sandra's tried. Becca's as straight as they come. She has a very serious boyfriend."

"And she came to a lesbian resort?"

"According to her, she was the one who suggested it. She said she didn't need to ruin her vacation fending off, in her words, 'sleaze balls hitting on her.'"

"But surely a few women will do the same," Kelly said. "This *is* a lesbian resort," she repeated, "and lesbians are everywhere, and she's very attractive."

"She gets hit on all the time when we all go out. It doesn't bother her. She politely declines and has a good laugh over it."

"And her boyfriend is okay with this?" Kelly asked.

"Oh, yeah. Kevin's a great guy. Sandra and I think he's going to ask her to marry him anytime."

"Will that change the relationship among you three?" Kelly had sensed the three women were tight-knit.

"Becca wouldn't let it. Her friends are too important to her. She dated this guy once who was stupid enough to say she needed to spend less time with 'those women.'" Matt used finger quotes to make her point, "and she told him to go piss up a rope."

Kelly laughed. "Good for her."

"Yeah. Neither of them takes any shit from anyone. They're the strongest, most confident women I've ever met."

"And you? Do you not take shit from anyone?"

"I try really hard not to. Sometimes I'm not the sharpest one in the room, but eventually I figure out what's going on."

"I'm surprised at that." Matt raised her eyebrows and looked at her. "I have no idea how I know that. It's just a feeling. Call it gut instinct." Kelly's gut was telling her lots of things about Matt, one of which was that she was an excellent kisser.

"Well, thanks, but it's the truth. I've also been told that sometimes I need to be hit over the head with a stick for me to catch on to something."

Kelly liked it that Matt could poke fun at herself, because not many people could. She could also take good-natured ribbing from her friends, which, in her mind, was also key to a great friendship.

Kelly thought about her friends. Since her breakup with Suzanne, they were few. Most had been Suzanne's and had stayed with her. The exception was Hillary, who had been outraged when Kelly had told her what she'd walked in on.

"She was what?" Hillary was a buyer for a large department store, and they'd met for drinks at a tavern not far from Kelly's house. Kelly lived near downtown Atlanta, in a forty-year-old house with lots of potential. She'd bought it and had spent the next two years renovating it to perfection. It wasn't long after she and Suzanne had started dating, when Suzanne began dropping hints that they should live together, and Kelly's place would be perfect. It was big, airy, and had tons of natural light. It was close to mundane things like the dry cleaners, grocery stores, and the nightlife Suzanne was so fond of. Even during the weeks she'd spent at Suzanne's house making love practically nonstop, Kelly had never been tempted to give in. She did, however, now know she'd made a mistake by giving her a key.

"In your house, in your bed, with Lorraine?" Hillary asked, shucking the jacket to her suit and tossing it onto the seat to her right. Hillary was, what she claimed as, geographically challenged, meaning she was barely five feet tall. She compensated by wearing four-inch Jimmy Choo's that made her legs look fabulous.

"Yes, on all points."

"Man, that sucks," Hillary said, shaking her head in disgust. "How could Lorraine do that to you? I really liked her. I thought she had more integrity than that," Hillary said.

"So did I," Kelly said ruefully.

"I'd never do anything like that," Hillary commented. "From either direction. That's just wrong."

Kelly didn't have anything to add.

"Well, I've known Suzanne for over ten years, but I can't be friends with someone who does that." Hillary put her hand on Kelly's arm. "I'm here for you, Kelly. Whatever you need."

Kelly's heart stopped. Was Hillary implying what she thought she was? Was she hitting on her three days after she dumped Suzanne? What was wrong with people?

Kelly's expression must have conveyed her thought because Hillary yanked her hand away.

"No, no, not like that! I mean you're attractive and all that, but that's not what I mean. I'm not hitting on you to get into your pants. God, no!"

"I realize that," Kelly said apologetically. "I'm sorry. I'm just jaded right now."

"No one can blame you," Hillary said calmly. "But that's not me. I'm your friend." Hillary laughed. "Well, I guess that word means nothing to you."

"I thought it did," Kelly said sadly.

"And it still does, to those that matter, those who are truly your friends. I guess it was a double whammy to lose not only your girlfriend but your best friend as well."

"You're right, but after I got over the initial shock, I realized I'm not terribly broken up over Suzanne," Kelly admitted. "I think that situation had fizzled a while ago." Kelly dropped her head into her hands. "God, and to think I told Lorraine I was having second thoughts about our relationship. She must have seen that as a green light."

"Don't you dare give her or Suzanne permission to do what they did. If you want out of a relationship, you say so. You can fuck whoever you want minutes later, but you always get out first. And you never, ever sleep with your best friend's ex. That's just not allowed in the lesbian friendship manual. Ick." Hillary underscored her last word with a shudder.

Doreen returned with their pizza, napkins, and two plates, pulling Kelly back from her thoughts. They chatted while they ate, and when Doreen came around again to pick up the remains of their lunch, Kelly declined another refill. She ordered water instead.

They spent the rest of the afternoon talking on and off about inconsequential things, and during several long stretches they had no conversation at all. Kelly was comfortable with only the sounds of people on vacation in one of the most beautiful places in the world. She people-watched, and a woman walked by with an orthopedic boot on her ankle. How was she going to get all the sand out of that? A few minutes later, another strolled by with a bright-blue cast on her right wrist. Kelly hoped that had happened before they came to the island, not during an excursion of some type.

Finally, she'd had enough sun for one day. The sand was white, the water crystal clear, but she needed to get inside, take a cool shower and maybe a serious nap.

Reluctantly she said, "I've got to go in. If I don't, I'll be worthless for the next few days." She gathered up her things and dropped them into her orange beach bag.

"I guess I'll see you around then?" Matt asked.

Kelly looked at Matt, and her body answered for her. "Count on it."

CHAPTER TWELVE

Kelly was talking to the concierge as Matt, Sandra, and Becca walked toward the lobby. They were catching a cab to go into town and wander around and find a place for dinner. Matt was suddenly nervous and tried to think of an excuse to go back to the room, but the sight of Kelly drew her in.

Kelly's hair was down, and she was wearing a sundress with spaghetti straps, exposing her newly tanned shoulders. Her sandals were flat and showed off her manicured toes. A small bag was slung over her right shoulder.

"Isn't that Kelly?" Becca asked.

Matt pretended she hadn't already seen her, and that her pulse wasn't racing like she'd just finished the hundred-yard dash in the Olympic finals. "Oh, yeah. I think it is."

"You're such a bad liar," Becca said as they approached. "Come on. Let's see if she has dinner plans."

Before Matt could protest, Becca and Sandra grabbed her by the arms and pulled her along with them.

"Kelly, hi," Becca said.

Kelly turned and returned their greeting, her gaze stopping on Matt.

"Ms. Howser, your taxi will be here any minute," the concierge said pleasantly.

"Thanks, Carol," Sandra replied, then turned to Kelly. "We're headed into town to grab something to eat." She jabbed her elbow into Matt's side.

Kelly was about to say something when Becca jumped in. "What our friend here," she tilted her head toward Matt, "would say if she had a brain in her head at this moment is, would you like to join us?"

Kelly looked at her, and Matt blushed with embarrassment. "I can speak for myself, thank you very much. Yes, would you? I mean, if you don't have other plans." Jeez, she sounded like she was asking a girl out for the first time.

"I don't want to intrude on your girl time."

"Nonsense," Sandra said. "We'd love to have you. Right, Mattie?"

"Yes, of course," Matt said suddenly, more than a little brain-dead. What had gotten into her? She was a successful author, but she could barely put two words together right now. She'd done fine earlier on the beach.

Kelly looked at Matt for confirmation. She was only able to nod. God, how virginal, she thought, mortified.

"If you're sure," Kelly said again, addressing Matt.

"Absolutely." Sandra poked Matt again. "Don't know what's gotten into our friend here, but she seems to be tongue-tied at the idea of having dinner with a beautiful woman."

Matt finally protested. "I am not. I just can't get a word in edgewise with you two around."

"Then we'll be sure to make ourselves scarce later," Becca said as their taxi pulled up.

"So, Kelly, tell us about yourself. What do you do for a living?" Becca asked after their waiter had taken their order. At the recommendation of their driver he'd dropped them off at a small restaurant tucked out of the way in a strip mall. Danny Bouy's, as the sign read out front, had the best fish tacos, the chilliest air-conditioning, and the coldest beer in town. Matt hated fish tacos and was the only one at the table to order something else.

They sat on the patio in front of the restaurant, their waitress arriving seconds later. Veronica was dressed in a referee shirt and shorts that Matt's grandma would describe as vagina shorts. The uniform definitely fit with the sports-bar theme catering to men.

"I'm an electrician."

The image of Kelly in a hard hat and climbing gear was sexy. "Like a climb-up-a-pole electrician or the come-to-your-house kind?" Matt asked, hoping to shift the focus off her lustful thoughts.

"I've done that, but no. I have a small electrical company, and we work primarily on new construction. We do some remodeling work, so, yeah. I would definitely come to your house. I wouldn't pass up the opportunity to see you again."

Matt's stomach flip-flopped at the not-so-subtle inuendo and the very obvious look of interest in Kelly's eyes. Sandra must have seen it too, because she bumped Matt's leg under the table. She was starting to feel in over her head, but it wasn't as scary as she thought it would be.

"How did you get into that? There aren't many female electricians, are there?" Matt was intrigued. "I'm sorry. That sounded really bad, but I admit I've never seen one."

Kelly laughed, making Matt's stomach do funny things.

"That's all right. Most people say the same thing. I got into it like anyone else. It caught my interest."

"How does one get to be an electrician?" Sandra asked.

"A few years of school, then a lot of hard work."

"I can do a lot of things around my house, but that I leave that to the pros. Too much chance to get hurt," Matt said. Her brain had begun to work again, and she didn't need her friends to carry the conversation.

"Most people think that way."

The waiter came with more chips and their second round of beers. When he left, Matt said, "So, tell me more about being an electrician. Tell me about your company."

"Well, I have sixteen employees, all female."

"Really? That's cool. How did that happen?"

"After my apprenticeship, I worked for a while for a company and got tired of getting hit on by everyone and being given all the shit jobs. Sexism still exists in the trades, unfortunately." Kelly looked like she had a bad taste in her mouth. "So, I struck out on my own. Pretty quickly I realized I needed an extra pair of hands, so I got in touch with one of the other women in my class and offered her a job. We hire right out of the trade school, and we've been growing ever since."

Even though Kelly's description of her journey was understated, Matt could hear the sense of pride in her words.

"That's what makes us so successful," Kelly said. "Women feel more comfortable with another woman in their house, especially if they're alone or have kids."

"That makes sense. Seems as though you found the perfect niche."

"I like to think so."

"Any plan on becoming a major contractor?" Sandra asked, ever the entrepreneur.

"I've thought about it, and it's an option, but not one I'm interested in at this point. That's a big commitment, and I'm not sure I want to go down that road. I like what I'm doing now. Anything bigger might just muddy the waters."

"Don't fix it if it's not broke?" Matt asked.

Kelly smiled, and Matt's butterflies ramped up again.

"Something like that. I'm a control freak, and since it's my company with my name on it, any bigger I'd lose control. And that would drive me crazy."

The image of Kelly taking control in the bedroom was exciting, and Matt tucked that thought away for another time.

"That makes a lot of sense. Where do you live?" Becca asked.

"Atlanta."

"Did you live there during the Olympics?" Becca asked.

"No. I moved there a few years after." Kelly turned her attention to Matt. "You know all about me, and I understand you two are the best friends on earth." She tilted her beer bottle in the direction of Becca and Sandra. "What about you, Matt? What do you do when you're not enjoying a vacation your friends sent you on?" Kelly settled back in her seat.

"I'm an author.

"Really? What do you write?"

"Children's books."

"I've never known an author. Are you famous? Would I know any of your titles?"

"Only if you're a preteen," Matt said comfortably.

"What kind of books do you write? I guess that's called genre, isn't it?" When Matt nodded, Kelly continued. "Are they like bedtime stories or Harry Potter kind of books?" Kelly seemed suddenly very interested in children's literature.

"Somewhere in the middle, actually. I have a series, and my heroine is a twelve-year-old girl named Dylan who can't keep her nose out of everyone else's business. She usually ends up in some kind of mischief solving crimes."

"That's way cool. I'm having dinner with a famous author. Do you write under your name, or do you have a pen name?"

"Under my own name, but I'm starting a new series about teenagers in the future. It's my first foray into sci-fi, and I'll use a pen name for it."

"Why would you do that?" Kelly asked.

"When people know an author, they expect a certain kind of book, actually in a specific genre. For instance, everyone knows Stephen King writes some bizarre, scary stuff. If he wrote a western, his readers would pick it up because he's the author but be in for quite a surprise after the first chapter or two. Readers expect a certain experience from an author, especially one who's written several books in that genre. For that reason, using a different name is pretty common in the publishing industry." Matt didn't share that she also wrote lesbian erotica, that she was pretty good at it and that it was very profitable.

"I never knew that," Kelly said, lifting her beer to her lips.

Visions of Kelly's lips other places flashed through Matt's mind, and she would have sworn she'd broken out in a cold sweat.

"Not that I'd have any reason to know, but it's pretty interesting," Kelly added, oblivious to Matt's plight. "How did you get started writing?"

"Kind of like you, I suppose," Matt said. "I'd always been an avid reader, and one day, I had some time on my hands and sat down with a pad and pen and just started writing." She didn't say that she was out on one of her pretend dates and was killing time until it had been long enough to go home. Becca and Sandra were babysitting and had made it clear Matt was expected to spend the night with her date. That hadn't happened, but the voluminous number of words that had flown onto the page had. Matt reiterated how she submitted her first book and how it was picked up immediately. Six others followed quickly, and while she was waiting for number seven to be published, she worked on her new series. She was more than halfway finished, the sequel already brewing in her mind.

"Don't forget about the lesbian sex books," Sandra said. Sometimes she could be a complete ass.

Kelly's eyebrows shot up. "Lesbian sex books?"

"She calls them erotica," Becca chimed in. "I call them hot."

"You have a boyfriend, Becca," Sandra said. "Don't tell me we're finally getting you to step over to the wild side." Sandra and Matt were always teasing Becca about her heterosexual lifestyle and often ended the teasing jabs with "But we love you any way you are."

"No, but I will tell you that I made Kevin read one, and I have to say…" She turned toward Matt, her face flushed. "Thank you."

"Me?" Matt asked, growing uncomfortable with the conversation. The last thing she wanted to do was talk about sex while Kelly was sitting across the table from her. "What did I do?"

"You gave me the best orgasm of my life." Becca used the menu to fan herself.

Matt dropped her head in her hands. "Oh, jeez," she groaned. "Can this get any more embarrassing?"

"Probably." Sandra jumped in. "Do tell." Sandra encouraged Becca to continue.

Matt jumped in. "Do not tell."

"Let's just say all of your books are a staple on my nightstand."

"Forget about the kids, let's focus on the grown-ups. How many of those have you written?" Kelly asked, an amused look on her face.

"Not enough." Sandra answered for Matt. "Unlike Becca's *boy*friend, I don't need any help in that area. But I can honestly say that the last woman I was with would probably say the same thing as Becca did."

"Can I just crawl under a rock anytime soon?" Matt didn't mind talking about her erotica, and both women were her beta readers, but to do so in front of Kelly was making her uncomfortable.

Kelly, however, was a good sport when she asked both Becca and Sandra, "What is one of your favorites?"

"Hmm. There are so many." Sandra was obviously mulling over the question.

Becca answered. "I'd say it's like kids. You love them all equally, but some are more interesting and exciting than others."

"That makes no sense," Sandra interjected.

"Can we talk about something else?" Matt asked, more a prayer than a question.

"Just one more question," Kelly said.

"At the risk of being completely mortified," Matt waved her hand as if to say go ahead.

"What pen name do you use for those?" She had her phone in her hands, ready to Google it.

"Alice—"

Matt interrupted Sandra. "We are not going there. My open book is closed." Matt cast a serious look at her friends.

"We're going to look around the shop next door," Becca said, standing and reaching for Sandra's hand.

"We are?" Sandra asked, then quickly said, "Yeah. Right. We are. Alice Monroe," Sandra said like a conspirator passing valuable information.

"What was all that about?" Kelly asked, watching them go out the front door. "Was it something I said?" She wasn't serious.

"No. Of course not. That's their not-so-subtle way of leaving us alone."

"Must have been all that talk about lesbian sex," Kelly teased.

"It's not sex. It's erotica." Matt protested but knew when she was beat.

Kelly swiped her finger over her phone screen, her fingers flew over the screen. "According to Google, erotica is defined as literature or art intended to arouse sexual desire. Potato, potato," Kelly said, using a British accent for the last word, making it sound like *pa-ta-toe*."

"Google doesn't lie," Matt said, suddenly finding it difficult to breathe.

"Did you want to go with them? They *are* your friends, and you *are* here with them," Kelly asked.

Something in her expression must have given Kelly that idea. Why else would she have asked? Did she herself want out of the situation Becca and Sandra had left her in? Matt swallowed. What was the saying in Vegas—go big or go home?

"No. I'd rather be with you," she said simply.

CHAPTER THIRTEEN

I'd like that too," Kelly said, her smile a thousand watts. Matt's heart beat a little faster and her clit got a little harder. Her hands started to sweat. She hadn't been alone with a woman she was this attracted to in a very long time. She decided to play it safe for a while.

"Other than being an electrician, what do you do in your spare time?" Matt asked, trying to calm down. That and she loved hearing Kelly's soft, smooth accent.

"I'm the sole owner of a women-only company in a very male-dominated field. What makes you think I have any spare time?"

"You managed to get here."

"True, and I'm glad I did." She looked directly at Matt, her message clear.

After a long pause, Kelly said, "Other than work and the rare trip to the grocery store, I play lacrosse."

"Lacrosse?" Matt asked. "Like run around with a net on the end of a stick trying to get a ball into a goal?"

"It's called the net, but yes. That's it."

"How did you get into that? Lacrosse isn't a common, everyday sport, is it?"

"I went to college on a lacrosse scholarship."

Matt sat back in her seat, the vinyl squeaking. "Really? Sorry. I didn't mean to imply you didn't look like the scholarly type, because you do. I just thought, that…"

"Because I'm an electrician, I didn't go to college?"

Matt wasn't sure if she detected teasing in Kelly's eyes or a challenge. "Um…" Matt felt her ship begin to teeter.

"I stepped into that one, didn't I? I'm such an idiot," Matt said. "That's not what I meant. I just assumed you went right from high school to being an electrician." Matt's ship slipped even deeper, but when Kelly finally smiled, Matt let out a sigh of relief as it righted.

"It's all right," Kelly said, her smile even broader. "Actually, everybody thinks that. Let's just say I was a late bloomer in discovering my true calling."

"Where did you go to college?"

"Smith."

"Smith College?" Matt could swear her voice squeaked.

Kelly nodded.

"Wow, beautiful, smart, and athletic."

"I worked hard."

"You certainly did. Isn't Smith back East somewhere?" Matt asked

"It's in Northampton, Massachusetts. About one hundred miles west of Boston," Kelly added.

"So, tell me about Smith."

"Most people think it's a bunch of snooty, rich white girls, flitting around sororities, going to frat parties at Harvard or Yale, trying to snag a rich husband."

"That's pretty harsh," Matt admitted, but then she realized that she too had that impression but just didn't express it.

"There were those, but most of us just wanted an excellent education. At least the group I hung around with."

"Was that the smart girls or the jockettes?"

Kelly laughed, a sound Matt wanted to hear again and again and again.

"Both. I was in the honors dorm, so we were a studious lot, and I needed to keep my grades up and skills sharp to retain my scholarship. My parents didn't have any money, so if I wanted to eat or buy mascara or tampons, I had to work. My scholarship paid for tuition, but that was it."

"That's admirable." Matt said.

Kelly shrugged off Matt's compliment. "It's nothing that other college kids don't have to do. I will admit, though, that I was one of the few that had a job."

"Where was it?"

"On campus, in the library. They worked around my schedule of classes and practices and paid me to sit around and wait for someone to come to the desk and ask a question. I spent most of my time studying."

"Tell me a funny story about your college life," Matt asked, eager to hear more.

Kelly tilted her head in a way that Matt recognized as her thinking look.

"For some reason the library was open twenty-four hours. Some nights I worked the overnight shift, and to stay awake, I'd bring my stick and ball and run up and down the aisles. You can practice a lot of moves sliding in and out of the aisles and zigzagging around the study carousels."

"That's good thinking." Matt wished she'd had that opportunity when she was in college. She'd worked her ass off at her measly part-time job.

"I never told anyone, and when practice started that next season, our coach was surprised at how much better I was."

"Did you ever share your secret with any of your teammates?"

"Yeah, I did, and most of them thought I was crazy. Sleep was always in short supply, but it was what I needed to do. I won the lacrosse player of the year three years in a row. So, who was crazy then?"

"That's a lot of work," Matt said, admiring her tenacity.

"Just a passion for the game."

"So, you play now?" Matt asked.

Kelly nodded.

"Are there teams, or clubs, or Saturday-morning pickup games?" She had absolutely no idea.

"No. Actually Atlanta has several leagues—one for men, one for women, and a mixed league."

"Let me guess. You play the mixed."

"Why do you say that?" Kelly asked.

"I imagine you're always up for a challenge, another level of competition. You want to better yourself, and playing against men gives you that," Matt said, not sure where that insight came from.

"Probably a little bit of all the above."

"So, you graduated from Smith. Then what?" Matt asked.

"I have a degree in history, so I got a job teaching in a high school in Atlanta and bought a small fixer-upper. I followed the electrician that I hired to rewire my kitchen, found a new love, and eight years later, here I am in a resort full of lesbians."

"You could be in worse places."

"There's no place I'd rather be."

Kelly was looking directly at Matt, and the not-so-vague sense of arousal she'd been feeling all day kicked up a notch.

"Would you like to head out down to the beach? I think we can catch the sunset if we hurry."

"I'd love to," Kelly replied, gathering her bag.

"I'm sorry if Becca or Sandra made you feel uncomfortable," Matt said as they stepped onto the boardwalk that snaked along the shoreline. The sun was setting over the water, casting the sky in a bright-orange glow. Kelly stopped and, with one hand on Matt's shoulder, slid off her sandals. The breeze blew Kelly's skirt around her knees, giving Matt more than a little glance at firm thighs.

Kelly's touch sent shock waves through Matt, and she reached out and grabbed the rail for support. Fire burned through her and stopped, smoldering between her legs. It had been a long time since a woman had touched her, and she was reacting accordingly. She hadn't realized how much she missed it until now. Her shoulder was suddenly cold when Kelly removed her hand.

"No, not at all," Kelly answered as they moved down the walk. "It's obvious they care about you."

"Sometimes a little too much." Most of the time Matt didn't mind, but when they started after her about going out and getting serious with someone, it was all she could do not to tell them to mind their own damn business.

"I love this composite decking," Kelly said abruptly.

Matt frowned. Had she missed part of a conversation? Was her head in such a sex haze she couldn't follow a simple conversation? "What?" She lived in Phoenix, where the only type of deck she knew of was the cement mixture of what was called cool deck around her pool.

"The planks aren't wood but composite," Kelly said, pointing at the horizontal slats under their feet as they walked. "They're made from recycled material, making them much more durable and with a longer lifespan. No worries about cracking or splinters on your bare feet."

"Wow, a three-time collegiate lacrosse player of the year, an electrician, and a know-about-decks woman." Matt's head had cleared from the fog that had engulfed it when Kelly touched her. They stopped at a vista that popped out from the boardwalk to their left, and Matt rested her hip against the rail, facing Kelly, their bodies inches apart. "Is there anything you don't know?" Her chuckle caught in her throat when Kelly tucked a strand of hair behind her ear, fire sparking in Kelly's eyes.

"What it would take for you to kiss me?"

Heat and desire flooded Matt's veins as she searched Kelly's eyes. They were expressive and, at this moment, mirrored what she was feeling.

Matt's heart hammered as she reached up and stroked Kelly's cheek with the back of her fingers. It was warm and soft, Kelly's breath brushing her fingers. Never taking her eyes off Kelly's, she moved to cup her hand behind Kelly's neck, threading her fingers through her thick hair. Slowly Matt pulled her closer and kissed her.

It had been a very, very long time since Matt had kissed anyone, and longer than that since she had quaked with desire like this. The instant their lips met, Matt felt like she'd come home from a long journey she didn't know she'd been on. It was the sweetest kiss, one that held promise, adventure, and excitement. One that would chase away her doubts, fears, uncertainty, and loneliness.

Kelly kissed her back, a low moan coming from somewhere. The sound was exciting, the feeling in the pit of her stomach and the tingle in her clit becoming more demanding.

Kelly slid her hands up Matt's arms and circled them around her neck as she pressed against her. Matt wrapped her arms around Kelly, rejoicing at the familiar yet forgotten intimacy. Matt's head swam with thoughts and emotions, all centered on Kelly. She wanted to kiss her for a very, very long time in all the right places.

As her knees threatened to give way, Matt pulled her head back, breaking the kiss. Their entire bodies and their foreheads were touching, and for a long time neither of them moved. Matt struggled to catch her breath.

"Well," Kelly said softly, her voice husky. "That was certainly worth the wait."

"Yes, it was," Matt replied, her own voice not sounding quite right.

Her body, long dormant from the feel of another woman, was responding in a way she thought it never would again when Kelly shifted her hips slightly. They fit together in all the right places, and a few specific ones had definitely come alive. Her nipples were hard where Kelly pressed against her, her clit begging to feel the pressure of Kelly's thigh. She clenched her jaw to control the overwhelming desire to back Kelly against the rail and have her right here, right now. She shuddered and Kelly gripped her tighter.

"Can we do it again?"

The instant before their lips met this time, Matt murmured, "I thought you'd never ask."

Matt didn't stop to analyze what was happening between them; she just responded. She was drawn to Kelly in a way she'd never been with another woman. She foolishly wanted to know everything about her. She had no worries about the future but just reveled in the present, this moment that felt so incredibly right.

"Hey, you two," Sandra's voice pierced Matt's brain, and she jumped back, leaving Kelly to grab the handrail for support. "People are starting to stare. Come on. Let's get both of you back to the resort, where you can have a little privacy."

CHAPTER FOURTEEN

K elly was still trying to get her body under control when the taxi dropped them off at the resort. It hadn't helped that she and Matt had been in a backseat so small they were almost sitting on top of each other. She burned where her body touched Matt's every time the vehicle turned a corner. If not for Matt's polite, outstretched hand, she probably would have stumbled as she climbed out of the backseat.

She had enjoyed herself this evening more than she'd expected. She'd wanted to spend more time with Matt, but the thought of sharing her with her friends made her feel like a third wheel. She'd relaxed when they made it a point to prove to her that wasn't the case.

She knew Matt was attracted to her, but she sensed a bit of hesitancy in her eyes. Was it because her wife had died? Was she still pining over her? That kiss on the boardwalk sure didn't give her that impression.

Kelly had kissed many, many women, but none had devastated her so completely as when Matt kissed her. She was more than a little interested in Matt, who had something about her Kelly couldn't describe. It was more than her enticing body, her charm, or how cute she was when she stumbled over her words trying to make conversation. She was captivating, which was completely unexpected.

"Good night, you two," Becca said after they passed through the lobby. She directed her next comment to Matt. "We won't wait up."

Her heart hammered so loud she was sure Matt could hear it, and she didn't want the evening to end. "Would you like to have a nightcap by the pool?" she asked.

"I'd love to."

Kelly took Matt's hand as they strolled through to the bar. The discreet lighting along the path to the pool was enough to see by without ruining the mood of a warm tropical night. The air smelled faintly like the ocean. They stopped at the bar, and Kelly took Matt's hand again and led her to a cabana in a secluded corner. There they kicked off their shoes and sat down, extending their legs. A warm breeze fluttered the canvas fabric overhead. Others were enjoying the evening too, but to Kelly, in the cocoon of the cabana, they seemed to be all alone. The moon was a sliver, the stars bright and blinking overhead.

Kelly was suddenly uncharacteristically nervous as they sat in silence sipping their drinks. The sound of the waves crashing in the distance echoed the churning in her stomach. She wanted to go to bed with Matt and was pretty sure the feeling was mutual. So why were they sitting here and not throwing back the covers in her room?

"Do you ever wonder what your life would've been like if you'd taken a different path?" Kelly asked, needing to talk about something to settle her nerves.

"In terms of what?"

"Oh, I don't know," Kelly said, struggling to answer her own question. "Maybe if you ended up with your first girlfriend."

"My first girlfriend or the first girl I kissed?" Matt asked.

"The first girl you kissed."

"That was Paige Bartlett."

"How old were you?" Kelly wanted to know all about Matt's first kiss. She knew she'd never forget her first kiss with Matt.

"I was fifteen. An awful age."

"Tell me about you and Paige Bartlett if you were together today."

Matt thought for a few moments. "I would probably be dead."

"Wow," Kelly said. "I didn't see that coming. Why? It would be an absolute shame, by the way, because then I wouldn't know what it was like to kiss you and have this wonderful evening with you."

"Thank you. One of her brothers probably would've killed me," Matt explained. "They certainly wanted to when they found out about us. They thought I was trash and had corrupted and seduced their sister, when it was actually the other way around. Paige wouldn't take no for an answer. I hadn't quite figured out that I liked girls, but I knew there was something different about me. I wasn't interested in the same things other girls were at that age. It never occurred to me that I might be a lesbian. Paige, seventeen and very sophisticated, was one of the popular girls, yet she never gave any indication that she was into girls. But the way she was after me was hard-core pursuit."

"And you were what she wanted?"

"Apparently so."

"And how was it?" Kelly asked. "When she caught you?"

"Fucking awesome."

They both laughed, and Kelly's heart flip-flopped at the sound.

"So, where does the death by brother come in?"

"Let's just say Paige liked to live life on the edge. She was very adventurous." Matt smiled at the memory.

"Do tell," Kelly asked, suddenly wishing she'd been Matt's first kiss.

"She was a little risky, and just being with Paige was thrilling. I was young, dumb, and horny as hell. I'd just found out that orgasms were the answer to the great mystery of life. We were behind the shed in her backyard when one of her brothers turned the corner at a very inappropriate time. Boy, did he get an eyeful. Of course, he blamed me, even though one of Paige's hands was under my shirt and the other down my pants. I ran as fast as I could and never looked back."

"How about you," Matt asked. "Who was your first kiss?"

"Monica Simpson. She was seventeen and I was nineteen."

"Nineteen?" Matt asked, obviously surprised. "As in one-nine *years* old?"

"Yes, nineteen. It wasn't like I didn't know I was a lesbian. I was just plain chicken." Kelly remembered how her palms got sweaty and her brain ceased to function whenever she was around a cute girl. Kind of like now, she thought.

"Well, judging by the way you kissed me on the boardwalk, you've certainly gotten over your shyness."

"Thank you," Kelly said, all nervousness now gone. "There's a lot more where that came from."

"Is that an invitation?"

"Depends."

"On?"

Kelly moved closer to Matt. The heat radiating off Matt's body had nothing to do with the warm, night air.

"On whether you can do casual, no-strings sex. We're both here for a short time, and then you go home to your life and I return to mine." Kelly saw the flicker of desire in Matt's eyes and more than a little hesitation. The kiss on the boardwalk was a definite yes, but now, when it came down to it, Matt obviously had some reservations.

"You don't need to decide right now," Kelly said, giving her an out if she needed one. Matt looked relieved. Kelly leaned down and kissed her. It was a passionate kiss, one that held potential and barely restrained desire. Instinct told her that if she pushed, Matt would run, and that was the last thing she wanted. Something inside Matt was struggling to get out, and Kelly was determined to be the one that held the key.

"Come on," Kelly said, pulling Matt to her feet. The kiss had left them both struggling to breathe. "Walk me to my door before I pull the shade down and make you really see stars."

Kelly held Matt's hand, not wanting to lose the connection. That was silly, because the current passing between them had nothing to do with electricity. She was in no hurry, so she led them on a meandering path back to her room. They passed several couples also enjoying the quiet evening, and one couple locked in an embrace oblivious to anything around them.

When they arrived at her door, the sound of the lock sliding open was unusually loud. Kelly opened the door and turned to face Matt.

"You are a very attractive, sexy woman, Mattingly Parker, and I'd love to spend the night with you." She was having a hard time keeping her eyes off Matt's lips. She vividly remembered how they felt on hers and imagined how they would feel blazing a path over her skin.

"Kelly, I…" Matt had a pained expression.

Kelly put her fingers on Matt's lips and shook her head. "Find me tomorrow." She replaced her fingers with her lips and kissed her, then ended the kiss while she still could.

CHAPTER FIFTEEN

W hat in the fuck are you doing here?"
"This is our suite," Matt answered but knew that
wasn't what Sandra was talking about.

Sandra said as much.

"I don't have to explain myself," Matt answered. Even if she did, she didn't know what she'd say. She was more than ready to follow Kelly into her room and not come out until it was time to catch her return flight. At least she thought she was, but something held her back. She'd have to figure it out, and fast, because she didn't want Kelly to slip through her fingers.

"Yes, you do. We didn't expect to see you until tomorrow, if even then."

"Well, I'm here now," Matt said, heading for her room. "And I'm going to bed."

"Oh, no, you're not." Becca said, again tag-teaming with Sandra. "What gives?" Matt didn't stand a chance, and everyone in the room knew it.

"Nothing gives," Matt said weakly. "I'm just tired and want to go to bed."

"The sooner you tell us why you're here and not with Kelly, the sooner you can go to bed."

"There's nothing to tell. We sat by the pool and talked for a while, and then she asked me if I could do casual, no-strings sex."

"And you said?" Sandra asked.

"I didn't get a chance to say anything. I must have hesitated too long because she kissed me good night and said she'll see me tomorrow." That was the Cliff Notes version and would have to do for now.

"That's it? You just left?" Sandra said, shaking her head. "Mattie, you are about to lose your lesbian card, girl. You had a hot chick all over you. No commitments, no awkward call-me-later expectations. You'll never see each other ever again. That is perfect sex."

"Give it a rest Sandra," Matt warned her. "I have enough shit to deal with. I do not need yours added to the top of an already heaping pile." And the latest turd on the pile had been placed there today—a text from her mother-in-law.

MIL: I hope you are enjoying your vacation away from Jordan. Translation: A good mother who truly loved her child would never leave him to go on vacation to a tropical island out of the country.

ME: Yes, thx, and I know Jordan is enjoying himself even more. He's wanted to go to camp for the past few summers. Translation: I'm a good mother, have never left him, so butt out!

MIL: When will you be returning again? Translation: A good mother who truly loved her child would never be gone long.

ME: On the 16th. Jordan will be home a week later, on the 28th. Translation: It's not like I'm not there with him.

MIL: Oh, okay. I thought you'd be home much earlier. Translation: A good mother who truly loved her child would absolutely never be gone at all, let alone that long.

MIL: How are Rebecca and Sandy? Translation: I know you and your bad-influence friend Rebecca, the ball-buster DA, and Sandra, the dyke-lesbian-in-your-face activist, are having orgies.

ME: They're great and say hello. Translation: They're working hard to get me laid, and they say fuck you. *Gotta run. The taxi is here to take us to the museum. Jordan asked for a book about Juan Ponce de Leon. He studied him in history.* Translation: I'm done with your checking-up-on-me bullshit, and I always think of Jordan.

MIL: Be careful. People do crazy things while on vacation. Translation: Don't come home with a sexually transmitted disease since I know all lesbians do is fuck each other.

ME: Will do. Hi to Harrison. Translation: Fuck off.

"Mattie, what is it?" Becca asked.

"I said it's nothing," Matt lied. "I'm going to bed. Good night."

Matt was surprised Becca and Sandra had let her off the hook so easily. She went to bed but didn't fall asleep, and after several hours of staring at the ceiling, she got up and went out onto the patio. The air was warm, a soft breeze blowing across the balcony. She moved the small bistro table around in front of her and put her feet up. Soft laughter and the sound from the waterfall floated from the pool area, and she leaned her head back and closed her eyes. She had great friends, and even though they could be a pain in the ass sometimes, she couldn't have survived Andrea's death without them. She remembered when they showed up at the house.

Matt had managed to call Sandra and Becca, both of them appearing twenty minutes later in her living room without knocking. They sat down on either side of her on the soft couch, and Sandra reached out and took her hand. They didn't say anything. Becca and Sandra just being there, in Matt's space, was enough.

"She was in the mess tent when a bomb exploded near the center of camp," Matt said, her voice scratchy. "When everyone else was running for cover, she rushed out and dragged a wounded soldier off the street and into a tent. She went back..." Matt hesitated, gathering herself. She could fall apart later. "She went back four times to get the injured, and on the fifth she was hit with shrapnel from a rocket that came in a few minutes later. She died instantly." Matt added that Andrea had used her body as a shield for another badly injured soldier, and, due to her selfless act, that soldier had survived. But that didn't matter. Andrea was still dead.

"She was a nurse, and that's what she did. It was who she was," Becca said quietly.

"And it got her killed." Matt couldn't hold back the angry words that had been threatening to push their way out.

"And it got her killed. She was doing what she loved," Sandra said. "You know that."

"And it got her killed," Matt repeated. "She was supposed to be in a safe zone." Matt knew there was no such thing, just like the phrase "peacekeeping actions" often meant gunfire and roadside bombs.

"It was a hospital. What kind of savages attack a hospital?" Matt asked in anguish.

"Cowards," Sandra replied. "Fucking cowards."

Jordan stirred, and as much as Matt wanted to hold Andrea's flesh and blood in her arms forever, she loosened her grasp. He opened his sleepy eyes and grinned when he saw his Aunt Becca within reach. He crawled onto her lap and fell asleep again.

"Why don't you make your calls while he's sleeping? We're not going anywhere," Sandra said, her voice soothing.

Matt brushed a lock of his fine hair off his forehead and kissed the top of his head. She inhaled his scent, drawing strength for what she had to do next.

Seven phone calls later she dragged herself into the kitchen. Sandra had shucked her suit jacket and shoes, and Matt's large orange apron protected her silk blouse from the remnants of Jordan's snack. What wasn't in his mouth was on the floor under the watchful eye of Pluto. Pluto never begged for food but knew as soon as Jordan was out of his booster chair at the end of the table, the floor was his.

"I made you some tea."

"Auntie Sandra cooked," Jordan said, as if it were the second coming of Christ. He wasn't that far off. Sandra's culinary skills barely passed boiling water and "heat thoroughly."

"I see that, buddy. Is it good?" Matt asked needlessly. The remains of bologna and cheese as well as the chocolate pudding on his cheek told the story.

"She cooks more gooder than you," Jordan said with a mouth full of pudding.

Sandra stifled a chuckle. Both she and Andrea had had to scold her from laughing at the things Jordan said, especially if they were inappropriate.

"She cooks better than me." Matt corrected him out of habit.

"And you say I'm worthless in the kitchen," Sandra said, wiping Jordan's face with a wet paper towel.

"The palate of a three-year-old is not difficult to please." Matt smiled, but the attempt made her face hurt. It would be a very long time, if ever, before it felt normal to smile.

Either Becca or Sandra stayed by her side, being there when Matt needed them and providing silent support in the background when it was appropriate. It took five days for Andrea's body to be delivered to Hanson's Funeral Home and another four to arrange her burial at the veterans' cemetery across town. Andrea was buried with full military honors, and Jordan was frightened by the twenty-one-gun salute, wrapping his arms tightly around Matt's neck, burying his face in her shoulder. Matt crumbled inside. Becca and Sandra were on either side of her, her parents next to them, and Andrea's family across from her. Everyone, including General John Shakey, Andrea's commanding officer, wiped away tears after the lone soldier in full military dress uniform played taps as Andrea's coffin was lowered into the dry desert dirt.

After two weeks, Matt kicked her friends out of the house. She had to move on, however painful and overwhelmingly lonely it was. Jordan kept Matt busy, but Andrea's side of the bed was cold and empty. The days were busy, but the nights were unbearably long as Matt lay awake, reliving Andrea's smile, the sound of her voice, the touch of her hand. She was lucky. The company she worked for had just been sold, and she was waiting for a large check of her share of the sale. At least she didn't have to worry about money at the moment.

On a rainy Sunday afternoon, Jordan was playing in his room when Matt suddenly realized that he was way too quiet, which was never a good sign with a toddler. She steadied herself for whatever she might find he'd gotten into. Just before she stepped into his room she froze at the sound of his voice.

"Hi, Mama. What cha doing? I'm playing in my room. I went to GMa's and Pop Pop's yesterday. We went to McDonalds and played on the playground." Matt's parents lived seven miles away, and Jordan visited often. They adored their first-born grandson.

Matt's legs threatened to buckle, and she stepped into his room. Jordan was sitting in front of a toy computer pretending he was talking to Andrea. Her heart lurched, and she had to grab the doorjamb to steady herself. A sob escaped from the hand that was covering her mouth. Jordan turned to look at her.

"Mommy, I'm talking to Mama. Come talk to her."

Her son's request was so genuine and heartfelt, she fell to her knees. Jordan scampered over to her.

"Mommy?" he asked, clearly upset.

Not wanting to upset him further, Matt pulled herself together. She gave him a quick hug when she wanted to grab him up and hug him forever.

"Of course, I'll talk to Mama with you." She scooted to the toy, and Jordan climbed into her lap. This was their standard seating chart when Andrea called.

"Mama, Mommy's here." He turned to Matt. "Say hi to Mama."

Matt could barely get the words out, the knot in her throat choking her.

"I'll just sit here and listen. You talk to Mama." Matt stifled a sob on the last word.

Jordan looked at her, clearly understanding something was terribly wrong. Matt managed a smile when she wanted to rail at the injustice of the world taking away Jordan's mother.

Matt shook her head, blinked a few times, and shook her arms to erase the images that hadn't made an appearance in years. Reminiscing about the past was not helpful, and she forced her attention to her earlier conversation with Sandra.

Was Sandra right when she said that Kelly was definitely into her and had offered more than Matt had been offered in years? If so, why had she hesitated when she'd had the perfect opportunity to follow Kelly into her room and close the door behind them?

She'd kissed Kelly on the boardwalk without a second thought. She certainly hadn't forgotten how to do that. Was she afraid to have sex? No. That was absurd. You never forget how.

You always remember the texture of warm, soft skin. The ease with which steady fingers slide effortlessly through wetness. How certain words whispered in the dark night can light up the sky around you. How an orgasm can start at the tip of your toes and explode out of the top of your head. How the world ceases to exist, and your entire center of focus is on one woman and one little spot.

She ought to knock on Kelly's door, right now. Wake her up and silence her doubts and fears with heated, passionate kisses. Pull her close, inhale her scent, caress her with her hands and mouth inside and out, until she begged for release. Taste her. She yearned to get lost in the once-dormant sensations that were now active. She needed to be carried away in the primal need of woman and woman. She wanted Kelly to make her forget about everything.

What was wrong with her?

Matt knew she was dreaming. She was in the twilight, somewhere between sleeping and waking. That place where you were looking down on the scene below you. Was this what God saw every day or the view a loved one had while keeping watch over those left behind? She hoped it was neither, because the view was definitely X-rated.

She and Kelly lay in the same cabana they'd been in earlier in the evening, but this time it was on the shoreline, water quietly lapping around them. The canopy was fully open, the stars winking at them. They lay, limbs entwined, with nothing but the warm night air between them. Their kisses were slow and deep, while their hands deliberately explored. They moved together, legs shifted, and firm, strong thighs pressed against warm, wet desire. Their movements became quicker, need overtaking leisurely exploration. Someone cried out. Someone moaned, a combination of pleasure and blissful pain. Limbs, once pale in the moonlight, became flushed from arousal. Lips explored; bodies arched with longing.

Dominance transformed into submission, control into surrender, restraint into freedom until finally, for a split second, a sharp intake of breath, a heartbeat, both women teetered on the precipice of a magic cliff. A place where you enjoyed the journey almost as much as the destination. A scene so incredible you wanted to stay there forever yet wanted to take that last step to the end. That instant when two people became one, and the entire universe ceased to exist as the world exploded around you.

Matt woke with a start, heart racing, breath coming in gasps. Frightened at the clarity of her dream, she opened her eyes, expecting to see stars overhead and Kelly's warm body covering hers. But she lay in her room, in her bed, sheets twisted, the ceiling fan slowly turning. In her dream, strong arms held her; a soft voice encouraging her to the next level of desire. In reality, her arms were empty, a void where heat, passion, and life had once been. Matt curled onto her side. She had never felt this alone.

Chapter Sixteen

Kelly opened her eyes and immediately closed them again and rolled over. "Ugh." The sun had snaked its way through a small space between the curtains and landed in the middle of her face. She risked opening them again, rising out of bed just enough to see the clock. Her stomach roiled, threatening to toss up the remains of her dinner and the half-empty bottle of Crown Royal she'd left on the living-room table.

"Ugh. Why did I do that?" The empty room didn't answer, but the dizziness in her head reminded her in fuzzy detail. She'd tried to find answers in the cocktail she'd fixed shortly after she'd closed the door on Matt. When she didn't find them in the bottom of the first one, she realized she wouldn't in the third or fourth but kept looking anyway.

Why had she turned Matt away? All the signs were there that Matt just needed a little nudge. A little something to put the decision in the palm of her hand. Normally Kelly would have jumped all over such an opportunity, but something about Matt, she wasn't quite sure what, held her back. Vulnerable was the first word that came to mind, yet that didn't quite fit either. It wasn't fright or shyness or anything else that would have led Kelly to believe Matt wasn't up for a little vacation sex. The kiss on the boardwalk certainly screamed yes.

Her stomach turned. She had to get some food into her, quick. She gingerly took a shower, careful not to move her head too fast, lest she fall and break something. Feeling slightly better, she walked past the café and toward the pool bar. What she needed was some good old-fashioned greasy junk food. Can't go wrong with a burger and fries to cure a hangover.

Three large lizards stretched out on the sidewalk, taking advantage of the warm sun. They didn't move as Kelly approached and only scampered away when she was almost on top of them. One was missing its tail, and she guessed that someone might have tried to catch him before he disappeared with his friends into the shrubs that lined the walk.

The same friendly staff members she'd seen yesterday were on duty at the bar, and she motioned to one of them for coffee as she sat on one of the open seats. To her left was a couple in their thirties and, judging by the way they couldn't keep their hands off each other, obviously very much in love or lust. She wasn't sure which. Neither wore a ring, but she would never wear one to the beach unless she wanted to lose it. On her other side, past an empty seat, was a woman in her sixties, oversized sunglasses on her face and a large pale-green floppy hat shading her. Her legs were tan, and she either walked a lot or spent some time in the gym. She was reading a copy of the *Wall Street Journal*. The WSJ? On vacation? Staying current on business and the stock market made her able to pay for this expensive place, Kelly thought.

The bartender slid her coffee in front of her, and she lifted it to her lips. Steam rose under her nose, and before taking a sip, she inhaled the strong brew and began to feel a little more human. After three or four cups, she'd be right as rain, as her dad would say.

Her parents would love it here. They loved exploring new places, and a lesbian resort wouldn't have stopped them in the slightest. Over fifteen years ago, when Kelly informed them she wanted to take Shelley Holland to the senior prom, her mother made a trip to the principal's office to make it happen. Her father had gone with her to make sure the guy at the tuxedo shop didn't give his daughter "any shit," and he'd even let Kelly drive his new truck that night. She couldn't have asked for better, more understanding and accepting parents.

Shrieks from the pool behind her stabbed her in the back of her left eye, and she closed both of them to shut out the noise. That was impossible, but she did, nonetheless. Yet having them closed didn't affect the stabbing in her head, though it did shut out some of the piercing-bright midday sun.

After placing her order, she pulled out her phone and scanned her email. She had two accounts—one for work, the other personal. She'd left strict instructions to her staff not to send her anything that didn't need her immediate attention and was relieved to see the only senders were requests for quotes, which she forwarded to her office manager. She quickly turned the device back off and stowed it in her bag.

"Good morning."

Kelly turned a little too fast, and her head spun. She put both hands on the bar to steady herself.

"Are you okay? You look a little green," Becca said, concern on her face. She'd taken off her sunglasses and was scrutinizing Kelly.

"Yes, I'm fine," she added when Becca raised an eyebrow. "Just need some coffee and something to eat."

"How are *you* this morning?" she asked, changing the subject. She didn't want to tell Becca that she'd polished of quite a bit of alcohol last night trying to get Matt off her mind. And, if truth be told, her body to shut down.

"Good," Becca replied. "Three strawberry daiquiris, please," she said to the bartender.

Kelly had the urge to throw up. She took a few deep breaths and willed her nausea to go away, feeling Becca's eyes on her.

"Are you sure you're okay?"

"Mm-hmm." Kelly doubted she'd go to hell for a little fib.

Becca looked at her for several moments, as if she expected Kelly to slide off the bar stool any second. Kelly kept a grip on the edge of the bar to prevent just that. "Thanks again for inviting me last night. It was a lot of fun."

"You're welcome. We're glad you came. What are your plans for today?"

Kelly didn't have any and told Becca as much.

"We're headed out on a catamaran this afternoon. Would you like to come along? Nothing special, just sailing around the islands. Mattie and Sandra might do some snorkeling."

The idea of spending more time with Matt was tempting. The vision of her in a swimsuit again was mouthwatering. But spending it on a boat bobbing up and down in the water made her stomach queasy.

"And don't say you don't want to intrude." Becca said what Kelly was thinking. "If you'd be intruding, I wouldn't have asked."

"What about Sandra and Matt? It's their vacation too."

"Sandra's always open to having a pretty girl around, and Mattie…" She paused as if thinking of the right words to say. "I know Mattie, and trust me." Becca winked at her. "She's all in."

"What time?" Kelly asked. She needed time to find some Dramamine—a lot of Dramamine.

They met in the lobby at one, and Matt seemed surprised to see Kelly. She gave Becca a "what the hell?" look, and Becca just smiled.

"Hey, Kelly. Glad you could join us," Sandra said, winking at Becca.

Kelly looked at Matt, who blushed when their eyes met.

"Yeah, hi. What a surprise." Matt glared at Becca.

Other than it was pretty obvious Becca hadn't told Matt she'd been invited, Kelly wondered why Matt looked so uncomfortable. Had she misread her interest? Not by the way she'd kissed her, she hadn't, but Kelly wasn't interested in playing these hot-and-cold games.

"I just came down to tell you that I'm not feeling well, and I don't think it's a good idea for me to be out on a boat in the sun all afternoon." The excuse was more than a little true.

"No, really, it's okay." Matt jumped in, stepping closer to her. Her eyes were questioning as they searched Kelly's face for any sign of illness. "It'll be fun."

Kelly put her hand on her stomach as if she were feeling sick. "No, but thanks again for the invite. Maybe some other time. Have fun." She couldn't get out of there fast enough.

"What the fuck was that?" Matt clenched her teeth. "Because you sprung her on me, I was caught off guard, and you embarrassed the hell out of her."

"Hey. Don't blame us for your social inadequacies," Becca said, rolling her eyes

"Us?" Sandra asked. "What's with the us? I didn't know she was coming either."

"Social inadequacies? I am not socially inadequate," Matt said. She felt awkward at seeing Kelly again, especially after her very vivid dream last night.

"You could have fooled me," Becca commented. "Obviously there's something between you two, and I was just trying to help. You can't get together if you're not together."

"Trying to help?" Matt asked, flabbergasted. "I don't need any help."

"It doesn't look that way where we're sitting."

"Becca, for God's sake, stop including me in your matchmaking," Sandra said. She turned to Matt, holding her hands up. "Mattie, believe me, I had nothing to do with this."

Matt took a deep breath and started laughing, and Becca and Sandra looked at her like she'd had too much sun. Her friends loved her and just wanted to see her happy. But she could take care of herself.

"Look, guys. Stop. I'm a big girl, and I know how to ask a girl out and how to get one into bed. I don't need your help."

"But you have only twelve days left," Sandra reminded her.

"I know, and I appreciate what you're doing." Matt gave each woman a kiss on the cheek. "Now go." She pushed them toward the waiting taxi. "Go have fun. I'm going to find Kelly and…" Matt didn't know what she was going to do if she found her. Beg, plead for another chance. Offer to kiss whatever was ailing her and make it better? "Just get out of here."

Matt doubted she'd find Kelly. If she were in her shoes, she'd hole up in her room, nurse her wounds, and plot her revenge. But then again, if she thought they were gone for the afternoon, and she wasn't really sick, why wouldn't she be out enjoying the sun and the water? Matt turned toward the beach.

❖

"May I sit down?"

Kelly opened her eyes and lifted her hand to block the sun. "I thought you were going snorkeling."

"And I thought you weren't feeling well," Matt said.

"Miraculous recovery."

"Look, I'm sorry for the way I reacted. I had no idea Becca had invited you."

"And if you had known? You would have, what, stayed in your room, pleaded illness, or maybe said you'd changed your mind?"

Kelly was obviously peeved.

"No. I would have spent a little more time getting ready. I would have put on my new suit, made sure I'd shaved really close, brushed my teeth again, and brought breath mints."

Kelly fought a smile, and Matt let out a silent sigh of relief.

"Breath mints?"

"So that when I snuck a kiss, my breath would be minty fresh."

"After last night I thought you'd know you don't need to sneak anything."

The more they talked about kisses, the more Matt couldn't take her eyes off Kelly's lips. "But it's more fun that way," she said, the tension of the last fifteen minutes dissipating.

Kelly's eyes traveled slowly up Matt's body, lingering in all the places that tingled whenever Kelly looked at her. Her nipples hardened when Kelly's gaze halted at her breasts. Kelly licked her lips, and it was all Matt could do not to sway into her. Kelly raised her eyes and pinned Matt with raw, hot need.

"Have a seat."

Lying next to Kelly, Matt lost all track of time. They talked about this and that and nothing at all, just enjoying each other's company. Kelly closed the book she was reading and turned to her.

"I'm going in to cool off. Want to join me?" Kelly asked, indicating the water.

"Absolutely," Matt tossed her sunglasses onto the table between them. She'd cast surreptitious glances at Kelly and, on more than one occasion, got caught looking. She definitely needed to cool off.

The water was perfect, a mix of refreshing and crystal clear. There were no rocks or shells to trip over, and her toes sank into the soft sand as she walked farther in.

"Race you to the buoy," Kelly challenged her, an instant before she dove into the water and started to swim. Not one to be left behind, Matt took off after her.

Stroke by stroke Matt matched Kelly's, and Matt touched the bright-yellow buoy an instant after Kelly did.

"Winner!" Kelly triumphantly raised her arms in the air. She was breathing heavily, trying to catch her breath.

Matt grabbed the ring around the base and pulled Kelly to her just as her head dipped under the water. It was deep, and Kelly needed her arms to tread water to stay afloat. Their torsos came together, and Kelly wrapped her arms around Matt's neck.

"I wasn't going to drown," Kelly said, her mouth inches from Matt's. "Or were you just using that as an excuse to put your arms around me?"

Matt knew Kelly wasn't in any danger. "No," she answered, not able to take her eyes off Kelly's lips. "I used it as an excuse to feel you next to me."

Kelly shifted just a little, her thigh sliding between Matt's. "I like the way you think."

The gentle rise and fall of the water was sensuous and matched the rhythm of bodies sliding against each other. Matt had an overwhelming need to kiss Kelly like she'd never been kissed before.

"Am I going to have to ask you to kiss me every time?" Kelly chuckled.

Matt didn't need any other encouragement, and she lowered her head. Kelly's lips tasted like ocean and sunshine and held the promise of much more. Kelly pulled her closer as their kiss deepened. Still holding on to the buoy, Matt slid her hand down Kelly's back and cupped her ass. Kelly moaned against her lips, spread her legs apart, and practically climbed up Matt's thigh.

Matt desperately wanted to have both hands on Kelly, but if she let go, they would surely sink. Worse yet, they'd have to separate to stay afloat. They bobbed in the water, and Kelly wasn't shy about how she felt in Matt's embrace.

Kelly pulled her head back, her breathing ragged. "We can't do this here," she said, glancing around. She loosened her hold, putting some much-needed space between them.

Matt had completely forgotten about anything other than the taste of Kelly's mouth, her soft breasts against hers, the throbbing need between her legs. She struggled to catch her breath and her senses.

"I suppose not." The last thing Matt needed was to have Becca and Sandra bail her out of jail for lewd conduct.

"We can take this back to my room."

Matt's breath caught at the clear intention in Kelly's words. If she had any doubt, the look of blatant desire in her eyes erased it. Matt's heart raced, her mind keeping a close second. It had been years since she'd made love to someone that wasn't Andrea. Could she do so without thinking of her? Would she call out Andrea's name when she came? See her face when she closed her eyes? The first time she'd tried had been a disaster, and she'd never tried again. Never wanted to risk it. Until now.

"Matt?"

Kelly was waiting for an answer.

"Race you," she said before swimming toward the shore.

CHAPTER SEVENTEEN

Matt and Kelly hastily gathered their things and tossed their towels into the bin next to the pool. Charise was on duty again this afternoon, and she winked at Matt as she hurried by. They didn't hold hands or exchange any words as they followed the sidewalk through the resort to Kelly's room. They stood next to each other in the elevator, and when the bell rang announcing Kelly's floor, Matt silently followed her down the hall.

Kelly's hand was steady as she slid the card key into the lock. Good, Matt thought. At least someone was calm about what was going to happen. She was a nervous wreck. Kelly opened the door and crossed the threshold. Matt hesitated slightly, then stepped inside.

Kelly's suite was similar to hers, but Matt saw only one bedroom. *Oh my God, the bedroom.* Her nerves kicked into overdrive. Was she really going to do this? Was she going to be able to do this? She'd read a lot about what sex was like after the death of a partner, and it was more than a little frightening.

"Matt?"

"What? Sorry. Did you say something?" Matt asked, embarrassed.

"I said I was going to take a shower and get this salt and sunscreen off. I'll just be a minute."

"O…okay," Matt stammered like this was her first time. It had been so long it felt like it was. Kelly kissed her, bringing Matt's focus back to the reason they were here. "Make yourself at home. I'll be right back."

Kelly kicked off her flip-flops, shrugged out of her coverup, and dropped it onto a chair. As she walked toward the bedroom, she untied her top and hung it over the doorknob. From where she was standing, Matt watched Kelly stop, step out of her bikini bottoms, and toss them aside. Matt's jaw dropped at the boldness of her action. Who was she kidding? They were about to get naked and have sex. There was nothing shy about that.

A moment later she heard the shower running, and images of Kelly naked, water coursing down her body flashed in Matt's brain. She imagined her hands filling with soap and gliding over her breasts, hips, and long legs. She pictured her head back as she rinsed shampoo from her hair.

Before she could think about what she was doing, Matt followed Kelly, then slid open the shower door. Kelly turned around, not at all surprised.

"Need any help?" The shower masked any nervousness in Matt's voice.

"Actually, I do." Kelly pulled Matt under the water and kissed her.

Matt's senses went from overdrive into hyperdrive. She slid her hands over warm skin, glided over curves and valleys, and grazed over the peak of Kelly's breasts. Kelly sucked in a quick breath and pulled Matt closer.

Kelly pressed Matt's back against the cool tile and made quick work of getting her out of her clothes. She dropped her head and flicked her tongue over Matt's nipple. It was Matt's turn to gasp with pleasure.

"You like that?" Kelly asked needlessly.

"Yes," Matt managed to say, her train of thought centered on what Kelly's mouth was doing. God, it had been so long, and it felt so good. Matt masturbated several times a month, but this was something she couldn't do. Her knees grew weak. Jeez, she thought. If Kelly kept this up, she'd come before she knew what hit her. That thought deserted her as Kelly's hand slid between her legs. Her knees almost buckled.

Kelly switched her mouth to Matt's other breast at the same time her fingers found her clit. She grasped Kelly's hair and pulled her even closer. Matt's orgasm started to rise from low in her belly. It would take only a second or third pass over her clit, and she'd come. She wanted to, needed to, but before she had a chance to think how embarrassing it would be to get off that fast, her orgasm shot through her.

Blinding light cascaded around her as wave after wave of pleasure filled every limb and pleasure point. She couldn't breathe, couldn't think, could only feel. And it was exquisite.

"I love it when a woman is so turned on she comes almost immediately," Kelly whispered in Matt's ear. She'd been hoping Matt would follow her into the shower and was surprised she actually had. When she'd suggested they come to her room, Matt had a scared look in her eyes, and Kelly wasn't sure Matt would agree.

As they'd walked to her suite, Kelly's mind had been on all the things she wanted to do to Matt. Matt had said she was a widow, and Kelly wondered what that was like, making love to someone else. In her case, she was emotionally free and clear of Suzanne, but what did Matt think about when she touched another woman? She doubted that kind of love ever died, but did Matt have it safely in a place where she could move on? Matt had told her it had been a while since her wife died. What was 'a while'? One year? Two? Ten? She hadn't been sure what would happen until she heard the shower door open. Matt shuddered against her.

"You okay?" she asked, her fingers still on Matt.

"Yeah. Sorry about that," Matt said, hiding her face in Kelly's shoulder.

"I'm not."

"It's been a long time, and it kind of snuck up on me."

"How long is long?"

"Long enough for me to be nervous," Matt admitted.

"Of me?"

"No. Of me."

Kelly pulled back, her face inches away from Matt, who wouldn't look at her for the longest time. Finally, she did.

"We don't have to do this."

"A little late for that now, don't you think?" Matt's shy smile was cute.

"That was just the beginning." Kelly hesitated. "That is, if you want it to be." She certainly did. Her clit was so hard, the pounding was echoing in her brain.

Matt studied her for so long that nervousness crept up Kelly's spine. She suddenly felt like she had swept Matt into this, and that was the last thing she wanted. She liked her, really liked her. She suspected she had some baggage, but at their age, who didn't? It was just a matter of what you did with it. She wasn't sure Matt had checked hers at the door.

Matt spun Kelly around and pressed against her.

"I definitely want it."

Matt's kisses were demanding, her hands everywhere. Kelly whimpered with desire when Matt's tongue circled her nipple, then sucked on it. Kelly had a direct hot wire from her nipple to her clit, and Matt's mouth was electric.

"I want your fingers in me." Kelly wasn't much of a talker when it came to sex, but she was wound so tight with Matt she didn't want to waste a second. She needed to come fast and hard. She'd do slow and leisurely the next time. She rose on her toes and gasped as Matt's fingers curled into her.

"Jesus." Kelly said, her level of arousal surprising. She usually couldn't come standing up, but if Matt kept doing what she was doing, she would.

"Yes, just like that." She thanked God Matt was a good listener, and her climax overtook her an instant later. Matt shuddered again, and Kelly kissed her, their breath mingling together.

They dried off, and Kelly wasn't sure if this was the end of their time together or just the beginning. She certainly knew what she wanted. She wanted Matt on the bed, covers on the floor, the sheets damp and mussed from their lovemaking. Matt was passionate, and if their shower sex was any indication, she had the power to make Kelly forget about absolutely everything except the way she made her feel. Her body hummed with residual orgasm and tingled with desire for more. She didn't want to scare Matt by asking her to stay, but she didn't want her to leave either. She glanced at the clock.

"I suppose I should go," Matt said, catching her movement.

"No," Kelly said quickly. "I mean, if you want to sure, but…"

"But what?"

Kelly took a deep breath, suddenly nervous. She was never nervous with women, and certainly not when it involved having them naked. But she didn't want to blow it with Matt.

"But I'd like it if you didn't." There, she'd said it. She watched Matt's face for any sign of reluctance or hesitation.

"You were looking at the clock. That's the biggest hint you want someone to leave," Matt said plainly.

"Not in this case. I was looking at it to see how much time we had left before your friends would be looking for you."

Kelly's pulse sped up as Matt dropped her towel and stepped closer. Her breathing quickened when she reached out and caressed the top of her breasts with the back of her fingers. Her head spun when Matt's hot, wanting eyes followed the trail of her towel as she pulled it loose and it slid to the floor.

"Hours," Matt said as she lowered her head and kissed her.

CHAPTER EIGHTEEN

Sensations flooded Matt as Kelly molded her body into hers. Soft, hot skin, responding to her touch, Kelly pulling her to her bed.

Matt reveled in the sensations of Kelly under her. Their kisses were hot, passionate, and deep. She dragged her mouth from Kelly's enticing lips to explore the smooth column of her throat, the curve of her neck, the sleekness of her shoulders. Matt cupped a breast, making quick swipes with her thumb across a hard nipple. Kelly arched into her.

"God, that feels good," Kelly said, shifting so their legs intwined.

Kelly's hands roamed her back, hot on her skin. Her nails trailed down her spine, part pleasure and pain. The heat between them rose, and Kelly's breathing grew quicker. Kelly took Matt's hand and moved it between her legs.

"Touch me." Kelly's voice was hoarse yet a gentle command.

Matt's hand slid over warm wetness, making her dizzy. It had been so long since she'd touched a woman. Too long since she felt the pulse of desire under her fingers, the power and ability to give pleasure.

Kelly's center was soft, and when Matt parted the wet lips, a rush of Kelly's desire flowed into her hand. She ran her fingers through the liquid and slid them slowly over Kelly's clit several times. She memorized every scent, every whimper, every twitch of flesh around her fingers.

"God, yes." Kelly moaned, and Matt fought to control her desire. She wanted to take her, hear her name screamed at that one moment of pure bliss.

"I need you inside me," Kelly said, breathless.

Matt slid one finger, then two into her warm center. Kelly's arms tightened around her, and she stopped breathing. Frightened, Matt started to pull away.

"No," Kelly said. This time her voice was strong. "More."

When Matt slid another finger into her, she was rewarded with another shudder of pleasure and a hoarse command to go deeper. She wanted to please Kelly like she had never been before.

"Yes...uh...just like that."

Kelly squirmed against her. She felt every beat of Kelly's heart in her fingers buried deep inside her. Matt sensed how close to orgasm Kelly was and backed off just enough to stay poised in the moment for as long as she could. She wanted to go slow and explore every inch of her. She wanted to remember this moment for as long as she lived. Her senses were magnified by the raw hunger of the woman in her arms. The way Kelly responded to her touch was the most exhilarating experience she'd ever had. Matt wanted her as hot and out of control as she was. She desperately craved to taste her. She needed to feel her hard clit pulsing with desire under her tongue. Erotic thoughts she believed she'd never have again flashed in her mind.

Matt slid down, their bodies slick with sweat from their desire. She trailed kisses over Kelly's ribs, her stomach, and a scar on her left side, just above her tan line.

"Where did you get this?" Matt asked, wanting to kiss away any pain Kelly had experienced. It took a moment for Kelly to respond.

"You really want to talk about that now?"

Kelly's face was flushed, her chest rising and falling, her nipples hard. Her hips were thrusting toward Matt's mouth, seeking release.

Matt chuckled. She was actually having fun as well as going crazy with desire.

"Maybe later." Matt bit the side of Kelly's hip.

Kelly opened her legs wider, and Matt used the fingers of her other hand to spread her lips, flicking her thumb over Kelly's clit. Matt snaked her tongue around her, grazing her clit, wanting to drive Kelly crazy. The time for teasing was later. Kelly grabbed Matt's short hair and pulled her closer.

"Lick me," she demanded. "I need your mouth on me."

Kelly's words were like gas on an exposed flame, driving Matt higher. Kelly gasped at the first sweep of Matt's tongue on her. Her hips thrust up, and Matt withdrew her fingers and wrapped her arms around Kelly's thighs, holding her still. God, she tasted good, Matt thought. She dipped her tongue into her.

"Faster." Kelly lifted herself up on her elbows. Matt stared into Kelly's eyes. She was watching her. Watching Matt pleasure her. God, that was hot.

Matt's orgasm quickly rose again, and she ignored it. With her tongue she explored where her fingers had previously been, savoring every scent.

"Fuck, that feels good." Kelly's voice was almost reverent. "Faster," Kelly demanded again. "Harder," she pleaded, and Kelly's legs tightened around her. Kelly whispered her name in gasping breaths as she quickened her pace, their eyes locked. Finally, Kelly stiffened and, with one last cry, came hard. Matt watched her become more beautiful as orgasm overtook her, mesmerized by the changes in Kelly's face. She had seen it earlier, the mask of concentration transforming into the glow of release. Matt knew she would never grow tired of seeing this woman come in her arms.

Matt watched in amazement as Kelly's breathing slowed. She had never been so content. A strong, beautiful woman lay in her arms, and Matt wanted, no, needed, for her to come again. Slowly she moved her mouth, and Kelly twitched in response. It took very little to push her over the edge once more. Matt held her close as wave after wave of pleasure racked her body. She was exquisite. Her little moans and soft whispers only heightened Matt's arousal.

Matt was insatiable and took Kelly over and over. It was when exhaustion threatened to overwhelm her that Kelly finally grabbed Matt's wrist and softly whispered for her to stop. Matt made a silent promise to herself. Whatever happened, she would never forget this day.

"You're damn good at this," Kelly said, obviously trying to catch her breath. "Come up here."

Matt didn't want to leave where she was, but she'd give Kelly anything she asked for.

She wanted to take the long road back up Kelly's body, exploring all the places she might have missed on her way down, but Kelly would have nothing to do with that. She pulled Matt up and into a passionate kiss, and she was instantly sailing on another wave of desire. Kelly smiled against her lips when she started to rub against her thigh.

"Not so fast this time," Kelly demanded, pushing her back onto the rumpled sheets.

This time Kelly took control, and Matt closed her eyes to simply feel.

"Matt. Look at me." Kelly said.

It took a moment for the voice to seep into her brain. She had to blink a few times to clear her head. Kelly's eyes bored into hers as if checking to be sure that Matt knew it was Kelly who was kissing her, touching her.

Matt raised her hand, and it shook as she touched Kelly's cheek. It was Kelly, not the ghost of a past life. It was this woman who had made her breath stop, her body break through into the daylight again after so many years in the dark.

Matt wanted to scream touch me, make me feel desired, make me forget about everything except how I feel when you touch me. Instead, one whispered word said that and a million other unspoken desires.

"Kelly."

Time after time Matt came, one climax stronger than the last. Kelly teased her, bringing her to the brink of climax, then backing off just enough to make her groan with frustration. She had never been as aware of the way her body responded as she did in Kelly's arms. Every nerve was touched, aroused, soothed, and aroused again. She was overloaded from the sensations Kelly brought out in her. Some were coaxed, and others exploded of their own free will.

The beginnings of Matt's orgasm rose again. Kelly's mouth was on her, and she desperately wanted to wait so this intensity would last longer. But she couldn't stop it. She grasped Kelly as first one, then a second shattering orgasm tore through her. Stars as bright as those sparkling in the summer sky beat her eyelids, accompanied by a kaleidoscope of colors. She was soaring as high as the clouds. This was the most powerful orgasm she'd ever experienced, a force that swept through her, washing away all her fears and her loneliness.

Slowly she emerged from the fog, her blood still racing, twitching all over. Kelly lay beside her, propped on one elbow, watching her. Matt still couldn't believe this wasn't a dream. Warmth spread through her as Kelly's eyes traveled over her. She had no idea where the covers were and didn't care. It felt good that Kelly liked what she saw, and Matt had no desire to hide from her. Kelly leaned over, cupped her chin, and kissed her.

Almost instantly, desire sparked again. Matt charted a trail of biting kisses down Kelly's neck and over her breasts. She took her nipple into her mouth almost in desperation. She swept her hands impatiently over Kelly and into her again. Kelly's breath quickened, and she threaded her fingers through Matt's hair.

Matt stroked her clit with her thumb, her fingers sliding in and out in time with Kelly's hips moving. She couldn't get enough.

"I can't help myself," Matt said, kissing Kelly. "You are incredibly sexy. You're so hot and silky, and I can't keep my hands off you."

"Do you hear me complaining?" Kelly choked out.

The pleasure of making love to Kelly was so intense, Matt wasn't sure she wouldn't implode. Higher and higher they climbed together, cresting seconds apart. Matt buried her face in Kelly's neck, her breathing choppy, her head spinning.

For a long time, neither of them moved. Gradually her head cleared, and she shifted, moving her weight off Kelly. She rolled over onto her back and pulled Kelly along with her. Kelly settled in, her head on Matt's shoulder, the soft weight of her arm across her belly.

"I hope I didn't scare you," Matt said nervously.

Kelly considered Matt's statement for a few moments. She'd been with many lovers, each different in her frequency and desires. None of her experiences had been as intense as the last few hours with Matt. Frightened wasn't the word Kelly would use to describe their time together. Powerful—definitely. Potent—absolutely. Urgent—at times, yes. But not frightening.

"No, not at all."

"I just…" Matt stopped.

Kelly sensed Matt's unease and rolled over on top of her, bracing her weight on her elbows. She looked into eyes that were troubled.

"You don't have to explain. I loved it. You're an exciting woman, and I want you again."

Kelly had an overwhelming desire to touch Matt and give her the same pleasure she'd experienced repeatedly. She kissed her hot and hard, and Matt instinctively moved under her. Kelly reluctantly dragged her lips away and kissed the fine bones of Matt's cheeks and along her jaw line before returning to the enticing mouth. Matt's hand roamed over her back, pulling her closer.

Kelly kissed her way down Matt's neck, stopping to tease the racing pulse just above her collarbone, then continuing her journey to taste Matt's breast. When she captured Matt's nipple with her mouth, Matt gasped and arched into her. Yet again, the heat and wetness of Matt's desire was evident as Matt pushed against her.

Kelly moved her hand over Matt's stomach in a gentle caress. The muscles under her fingers quivered as she continued her path downward. She nipped Matt's nipple as she settled her hand between Matt's thighs. She moved her fingers ever so slightly, and Matt arched her back as she groaned.

"God, that feels good."

"You are so warm." No matter how many times Kelly had touched Matt already, she continued to be in awe as she delicately traced Matt's folds, just barely grazing her clitoris.

"Do you like that?" Kelly asked. She knew what Matt liked, but Matt answered her anyway.

"Oh, yeah," Matt growled, her voice thick with desire.

Kelly needed her mouth on Matt. Needed to taste her desire, feel her pulse under her tongue, breathe in her scent. Kelly gently touched the bright-red surface with her tongue.

Matt gasped again, her breath coming in quick gasps. She started to move in time with Kelly's exploring tongue and suddenly arched upward as she rode the crest of desire. "Oh God, Kelly!"

CHAPTER NINETEEN

I t's about time you got home, young lady."

The pink rays of dawn were barely streaking through the sky when Matt had walked back to her room. The same man had been pushing the water off the sidewalk with his squeegee and greeted her with a knowing smile. The things he must see, Matt thought.

She leaned against the wall while she waited for the elevator to arrive. She was dead on her feet but was humming with energy. Women were made for having sex with women. They could make love all night, and she was lucky Kelly was not a one-and-done girl. It had been like they had discovered pleasure for the first time and would never experience it again once the sun rose.

The quiet ding of the elevator roused her from her stupor, and Matt stepped inside and pushed the button for her floor. Their room was on the third floor, and she usually took the stairs, but every muscle in her body was spent, in her legs particularly. Kelly had been an amazing lover, drawing more and more out of Matt than she could ever imagine.

"Do you have any idea what time it is, Mattingly Christina?" Becca said, pretending to scold her.

She hated it when Becca used her full name. Her mother had done that when she was in trouble…big trouble. "Time for me to go to bed," Matt replied.

"I think you've had enough time in bed," Becca said, spot on in her assessment.

"That's why I need to get some sleep."

"Not until I hear every detail of your night." Becca pointed to the chair across from the couch where she was sitting.

"Spill."

"Get Sandra out here." Matt stifled a yawn. "I'm going to tell this only once." Matt sat, knowing the sooner she answered their twenty questions, the sooner her head could hit the pillow.

"Sandra hooked up with the sweet redhead she was after all afternoon. No, wait." Becca paused for effect. "You wouldn't know about that because you were with Kelly all afternoon and evening and night."

"Mom, you didn't wait up, did you? I'm a big girl." Matt's tone was snarky. Becca was under a blanket, a cup of coffee in her hands. She didn't look like she'd been awake all night.

"And if I did?"

Matt suddenly felt guilty. The walk of shame of coming home in the same clothes you left in the night before was bad enough.

"I sent you a text," Matt said apologetically.

"Yes, you did, and no, I did not sit up all night waiting for you. I'm an early riser, and this morning was just a bit earlier than usual. I'm only on my first cup of coffee." She held up a green-and-white mug. "Now that we have established my timeline and the whereabouts of our roomie, spill."

Matt loved her friends and they shared everything. Well, almost everything. She hadn't told them she hadn't had sex since Andrea was deployed more than six years ago.

"I was with Kelly." Just the mere speaking of her name brought back flashes of images of bodies twisting in the dark, reaching out for contact, overwhelming desire, sighs of passion, cries of ecstasy. She was hot all over again. She managed to get up without drawing too much attention to the soreness in her legs and grabbed a bottle of water from the fridge.

"Tell me something I don't know," Becca said on her way back.

"It was nice."

"The way you blushed when you said her name and the fact that you came in at five a.m. and can barely move says it was more than just nice." Becca used air quotes to emphasize the word. "That and you have that fucked-all-night look on your face."

"Guilty." Matt held her hands up in surrender. "Now that you know everything there is to know, I'm going to bed."

Becca shifted and patted the cushion near her feet. "Sit."

"I thought you told me to spill. I spilled. Now you want me to sit? Make up your mind." Matt knew Becca would prod and pry until she got the info she was looking for, and that made Matt uncomfortable. She didn't want to analyze what had happened or share it with anyone. She just wanted to savor it a bit longer before any guilt or recriminations arrived on scene.

"Talk to me, Mattie," Becca said in a soothing voice.

"Is that the voice you use to get confessions out of little old ladies who jaywalk?"

"No. It's the voice I use when my best friend just had a very emotional event happen in her life."

Matt widened her eyes.

"Don't bullshit a bullshitter, Mattie."

Becca always had a way with words.

"I know getting back into the swing of things since Andrea's been gone has been tough. But I think this is the first time you've stayed all night. That's a big deal."

No, but what's a bigger deal is that this is the first time I've had sex in over six years, Matt thought. And I didn't feel anything or think of anyone other than Kelly, other than the first, last, and only time she'd tried.

It had been almost four years after Andrea died before she finally felt ready to start dating. It wasn't that she was still heartbroken over Andrea, but raising an active toddler alone, and holding down a job and managing a house, was exhausting.

Two years ago, she'd met someone in the school parking lot when she was waiting for Jordan to return from a field trip to the zoo. Her name was Tracy, and she was stunning. They chatted every day, and Matt finally got up the nerve to ask her to dinner.

Their date had been enjoyable, as had the four that followed. Jordan and Tracy's son were at a birthday sleepover, and both weren't due home until the next day. Matt had been edgy all evening. Neither she nor Tracy said anything about their free night, but Matt had thought about little else for days. She needed to get back into the dating pool, and as much as she loved Andrea, she was only thirty-five and way overdue for some release provided by something or someone other than herself.

Tracy had invited her in when Matt pulled into her driveway after dinner. They were both adults and knew exactly what would happen if she accepted. Matt was nervous, like a virgin, as she followed Tracy inside.

Tracy hadn't wasted any time, and Matt found herself backed up against the front door seconds after Tracy closed it. Instinct kicked in, and soon their clothes were on the floor, and they were lying naked on the couch. Matt was jolted back to reality when cold air hit her. She opened her eyes and found Tracy standing over her, pulling on her pants.

"I think you better go." Her voice was harsh, her breasts heaving as she tried to catch her breath.

"What?" Matt had asked, completely confused, her mind in pre-orgasmic mush.

"I said you need to go."

Matt struggled to sit up, searching for a clue to what just happened.

"My name isn't Andrea." Tracy's voice was flat, her eyes hard.

No number of apologies or explanations made a difference, and Matt had taken the coward's way out and never tried again.

"I'm handling it," she said, then added, "Really. I'm okay. Actually, I'm more than okay. It was fun, and we're meeting for lunch today. If things continue to go well, you may not see much of me."

Becca looked at her with her DA eyes, and Matt almost buckled and told her it had been one of the most meaningful events in her life. She'd gone places she never thought she would again and more than a few that she'd never even imagined. Matt wanted to stay here, cocooned from her in-laws, obligations to Jordan, and everything else that made having a normal, healthy sex life next to impossible.

"That was my assignment on this trip, wasn't it?" Matt asked before Becca had a chance to say any more. She stood and kissed Becca on the cheek. "So, if you intend for me to continue to get an A+ in my work, I've got to get some sleep."

Matt hustled out of the room and into hers, closing the door behind her. She stripped off her clothes, left them on the floor, pulled the covers back, and slid into the cool sheets.

Images of Kelly flashed through Matt's brain as she closed her eyes. The warmth of her body under her, the way it reacted to her touch, the soft caresses and demanding fingers coaxing her senses to life, the way Kelly used her tongue to trace a warm wet path up and down her body. Matt's clit began to throb.

"Jesus, Mattingly, stop acting like a horny teenager," she said aloud. "Close your eyes and get some sleep, or you won't be able to get any more of where all that came from." Matt focused on her breathing and tried the relaxation techniques she'd learned shortly after Andrea's death. They'd always worked to put her instantly to sleep. This time, however, as she thought of each muscle in her feet, the arch of her foot, the muscles of her calf, she pictured Kelly's tongue tracing every spot. She rolled over and prayed sleep would come.

CHAPTER TWENTY

Matt looked at her watch for the third time in half that many minutes. When she'd left Kelly this morning, they'd agreed to meet in the lobby at one for a late lunch. She'd pretended to be asleep when either Sandra or Becca opened her door to check on her, and when she finally got up, they were gone.

Matt wasn't up to the questions she knew her friends would bombard her with. The evening had been so intense, she wanted to keep it to herself for as long as she could before opening it up to the world. Well, not really the world, but Becca and Sandra, who, along with Jordan, were her world.

A pang of guilt hit her in the stomach when she realized that she hadn't thought about Jordan in hours. It was more like twenty-four, but she didn't want to count that high. She'd been so preoccupied with Kelly—her smile, the sound of her voice, her hands, her lips, her tongue—she'd thought of nothing else. Take away several more checkmarks in the mother-of-the-year tally box, she thought.

It was 12:57, and Matt was more than a little nervous. They'd made love all afternoon and into the evening yesterday, and when Matt had left a little before dawn, she was exhausted. Kelly had to be as well.

"Can I help you with anything, miss?" the concierge asked.

Every member of the hotel staff was friendly, always saying good morning or hello as they passed.

"No, thank you. I'm just waiting for someone," Matt replied, trying not to pace. It was another beautiful day, not too hot, and a light breeze kept the humidity at bay.

"I hope I didn't keep you waiting too long?" Kelly asked, coming up beside her and kissing her on the cheek. She slid her sunglasses from her nose to the top of her head.

"No. Right on time," Matt answered, not needing to look at her watch.

"I forgot my sunglasses and had to run back."

"You're definitely going to need those on a bright day like today." *On a bright day like today? Jeez, Mattingly. Could you get any stupider?*

"You up for riding bikes into town? It's about a fifteen-minute trip." Matt had asked the concierge about the bikes while she was waiting.

"Sure. That sounds like fun."

Matt turned to the concierge. "We'd like to check out two bikes."

"Certainly, miss," the woman replied politely. She reached for a tattered, blue, three-ringed binder, opened it, and flipped a few pages, then handed Matt a pen.

"Just sign for them right here." She pointed to the paper.

Matt followed the instructions at the top of each column header, indicating her room number, the number of bikes, and the current time. She spun the binder back around to face her.

The woman didn't even glance at her entries, just closed the cover. "Feel free to pick out one that suits you, and enjoy yourself. Remember that we drive on the left," she said, a large smile on her face.

"Do we need helmets or a lock?" Matt asked, a perfectly appropriate question.

"No. Not at all. Just park them by the shop you're going into. They'll be perfectly safe."

Matt looked at Kelly, who shrugged. This was a very different country indeed.

They approached four racks of bikes, which held oversized beach cruisers. They had two colors to choose from and multiple sizes. All had the hotel logo on the frame and a basket attached to the front handlebars. Kids had several smaller sizes to choose from.

Kelly wheeled one halfway out of the rack. "This looks about right," she said, backing the white one she'd chosen from its spot. With both hands on the black hand grips, she swung her leg over the red seat.

Matt chose a teal-green one, but hers had a black seat that had seen too much time in the sun. It was faded but still in good condition.

Kelly shrieked as she started to pedal, clumsily steering her bike across the sidewalk and into the parking lot.

"Oh my God. I'm so out of practice." She laughed as her bike wobbled a few times before straightening up. Memories of Kelly's laughter and giggles turning into sighs of desire commanding Matt to take action made her clit throb.

"Are you okay?" Kelly asked when Matt hadn't moved to get on her bike. She was probably standing there with her mouth hanging open.

"Yeah, sure," she replied, but she wasn't. They were both laughing as they headed in the direction of the main road.

"It's been ages since I've been on a bike," Kelly said as she hit a small pothole in the asphalt. She wobbled, and Matt was afraid she might topple over, but she straightened up without mishap.

For Matt it had only been a few weeks since she and Jordan had taken their bikes on an eight-mile mountain trail. Once a month she and Jordan met some of his friends and their families, each group taking a turn picking the trail. Inevitably, Matt was usually the only woman on the ride and often left the men to eat her dust.

"I guess it's true when they say it's just like riding a bike. You never really forget how," Kelly said.

Just like the sex I had last night.

"I'm pretty sure I'm going to feel this tomorrow," Kelly commented.

Again, just like the sex I had.

They followed the signs on the bike path that pointed the direction into town. The island didn't have stop lights, just a series of roundabouts, and with cars coming in every direction, Matt had to concentrate to maneuver safely. She could smell the ocean, and the tall beach grass sprouting up in the white sand on the undeveloped lots thinned as they got closer to town.

They parked their bikes in front of a small souvenir store at the first set of buildings they came to.

Matt was grateful to get off her bike without dumping it on the side of the road. It had taken a few moments for her muscle memory to kick in, but that wasn't why she had trouble keeping to the trail. Kelly was in front, her tight shorts and tank top providing an unobstructed view of her muscles as they pushed the pedals up and down. She came very near crashing into a light pole as her mind wandered to an image from last night of her riding Kelly's ass to climax and reaching around to bring her along.

"You okay?" Kelly asked.

Matt flushed at the memory. "Yeah. Just a little out of shape." A tiny fib, but she hoped it would explain her red face. She used the toe of her boat shoe to push the bike's kickstand into position. Matt stepped forward to get away from Kelly's scrutiny. "Let's go in and see if they have any cold water. I'm thirsty." What she really needed was to pour it over her head and down the front of her pants.

They wandered the aisles picking up a trinket here and there but not buying anything other than two bottles of ice-cold water. Then they went outside and sat on soft grass under a large tree, its canopy of limbs shading them from the intense sun.

"You handled your bike like you were a pro," Kelly commented.

Matt had a hard time focusing on what Kelly was saying as she tipped her head back to let the water slide down her throat. A lone bead of sweat snaked its way down the side of her neck, and Matt was finding it hard to breathe.

"Are you all right?" Kelly asked again, a knowing look in her eyes.

"Yeah, fine," Matt replied, probably a little too fast. "Just enjoying the view. It's beautiful here," she added as an afterthought.

"It is, isn't it?"

The way Kelly was looking at her, Matt wasn't sure either of them was talking about the weather. The light breeze blew strands of Kelly's hair across her face, so she reached out and tucked it behind her ear, the move so intimate it jolted her.

Matt stood up and broke the silence. "I'm hungry. Let's keep going and find someplace to eat."

She offered her hand to Kelly, and when they touched, a jolt of heat shot through her and settled in her stomach. If it had gone any farther south, she might have pulled Kelly back down, this time on top of her and not beside her. But Kelly stood, and Matt reluctantly released her hand as they walked toward their bikes.

Several stops later they came to another stretch of shops, this one much larger than the others. They pedaled past a pet store, a realtor, a tattoo shop, and three small specialty-clothing stores. Matt pointed to a sign that proclaimed *BIG AL'S BIKES, BURGERS AND BEER* on a large sign above the front door.

"How does this place look?"

"Heavenly," Kelly replied. "Especially the beer part."

It was a little too warm to sit at the tables out front, and after they parked their bikes in the bike rack, they stepped inside. A blast of air-conditioning hit Matt full force, and she sighed with relief.

"Oh, man, that feels good," she said, removing her sunglasses. The other stores they'd stopped at didn't have air-conditioning, choosing to rely on the naturally mild weather, but the island was having an unusual warm spell today.

The restaurant wasn't large, and inside to the left was a small bike shop with various styles of bicycles hanging on hooks from the ceiling. Once her eyes adjusted to the light, Matt saw that the area also contained several racks of shirts, shorts, and bike accessories. Boxes of helmets were stacked next to a glass cabinet containing high-end sunglasses. The shop smelled like bike grease and new tires.

"Wow. Never expected this." Matt stepped around her, heading toward one of the bikes hanging above their heads. She turned the price tag around. "Ouch." She grimaced and left the white tag spinning. "I'll come back and look around after we eat. Maybe I can afford a sticker or something," she said wryly.

"Have a seat anywhere, ladies," a booming voice said from their right. Matt turned, and a big, dark-skinned man wearing a too-large T-shirt was waving them toward the tables.

"Where would you like to sit?" she asked Kelly.

The dining area contained tables and chairs for either two or four, some pushed together for larger parties. Booths with red cushions lined the wall adjacent to a large bar, with another half a dozen running along the windows. They had their choice since only one other space was occupied.

"Let's sit by the window." Kelly pointed to a booth in front of a large window.

The waiter took their drink order, and when he placed their beers in front of them, Kelly spoke.

"You could have stayed for breakfast, you know."

Kelly didn't have to explain what she was talking about. Though Matt had left her room and gone back to her suite shortly before dawn, she'd thought about staying. But she had needed some space and time to get her head around everything that had happened.

"I know." Matt was unsure what to say next and struggled for the right words. No way was she going to tell Kelly that she was the first woman she'd had sex with since her wife died. Kelly made her heart gallop, her pulse race, and her head explode. She made her feel again. Matt had wanted those long-dormant feelings to go on forever, her drought unquenchable. This situation was unsettling. She absolutely would not tell her all that. It would be like telling her she'd taken her virginity, and that was heavy stuff.

Matt wasn't confusing great sex with love; she knew better than that. Before she met Andrea, Matt had had a lot of casual sex. It didn't mean anything, just a natural bodily reaction to a mutual attraction.

"How long ago did your wife die?"

Matt physically jerked.

"I'm sorry. I shouldn't have asked that question. It's none of my business."

"No. It's fine. Not many people actually ask."

"It was really insensitive. Again, I'm sorry."

"It's like people are afraid that if they bring it up, it'll make me sad." Until the last few years, Matt had thought of Andrea every day. Lately it had only been now and then. She would never forget Andrea and what they'd had together, but her name wasn't in every breath she took anymore. "It's been a little over six years,"

"How long were you together?" Kelly asked, her tone soft.

"Nine years. We met in college."

"Is it difficult to talk about her?"

Matt must have hesitated too long, because Kelly said, "I seem to be saying all the wrong things."

"No. It's all right." Matt smiled, reached across the table, and took Kelly's hand. "It's not that. It just seems a little weird to be talking about my dead wife with the woman I'm currently sleeping with."

"Have you never talked about her before with other women?"

Kelly had no idea there had never been any other women.

"Not really. I'd rather focus on the present than the past." Matt hoped this was a reasonable explanation.

"I'm sorry if I was a little clumsy." Matt knew she was blushing. "I was a little out of practice," she said, a large exaggeration of the truth. She didn't think she had been, but still felt the need to offer an explanation. Kelly gave her one of her sexy, sultry looks that made her clit tingle.

"Oh, you were far from clumsy." Kelly's voice was husky. "You knew exactly what to do, when to do it, and how to do it."

That was a relief, Matt thought. She didn't think she'd been all that bad. But as out of practice as she was, she still wondered.

"I wasn't hinting for a compliment," she replied, embarrassed.

"I know. That's why I said it. I was just reiterating how fabulous you made me feel in words instead of moans and sighs and screaming your name."

Kelly's eyes burned, and Matt found it hard to breathe. This scene was almost surreal, like she was in a dream—a very vivid one, and she didn't want to wake up. Not yet, at least. That would come when she got on her return flight.

"How are you?"

Kelly seemed surprised.

"Me?"

"Yeah, you." Matt smiled comfortably for the first time since sitting down. "I'm afraid I may have worn you out."

Kelly's face flushed, and her insides warmed at the memory of what had just happened. "Don't you worry about me. There's plenty where that came from."

Matt was tempted to call for the check and race back to Kelly's room for more of "that" but signaled the waiter over instead.

"I think we need to eat first."

CHAPTER TWENTY-ONE

How long had you and the idiot Suzanne been together?" Matt asked Kelly after the waiter removed their plates and they each ordered another beer.

"Three years." Why did it seem like much longer, Kelly asked herself.

"Did you see it coming?"

"No, but looking back on it, I'd say it was a waste of a couple of years. The first year was good. Everybody's is." Kelly toyed with the label on her beer. "All you do is fuck in every place and position imaginable. There's nothing wrong with that, of course. We didn't live together, thank God. Something nagging in the back of my head stopped me from making that commitment. Eventually she stopped pushing, and, I guess, we just were. Until we weren't."

"Sorry for asking. It's really none of my business."

"No. It's okay," Kelly said. "Pretty quick I realized I wasn't that broken up over it. Lorraine, on the other hand, is crushing."

"That's the ex-best friend?"

Kelly nodded. "I keep asking myself how she could have done that. Even if Suzanne came on to her, she should have said no. She should have told me, for Christ's sake. If your friends can't tell you the truth, what good are they? Isn't that in their job description? Even if she didn't want to tell me, she still should have said no. Who sleeps with their best friend's girlfriend?"

Matt didn't answer, Kelly's questions more rhetorical.

"I just don't get it. That's what I struggle with the most. It's not Suzanne. You don't go after your girlfriend's friends. Obviously, she didn't read that chapter in the lesbian manual. I mean, this morning, Lorraine called again and left a long message. 'It's not what it looks like, blah, blah, blah. 'I didn't mean for it to happen,' yada, yada, yada. I didn't see any gun to her head. I had no idea how long it had been going on, and I don't want to know."

"What did you do? When you found them?" Matt asked. "I probably would have killed someone, and it probably would have been a toss-up as to who."

Suzanne had a key to her place, and Kelly had come home early intending to surprise her with courtside tickets for the basketball game that night. She was getting a bottle of water from the fridge when she heard noises coming from her bedroom. As she walked down the hall, she knew exactly what she was hearing. It was the same sounds and words Suzanne always said when she was about to come.

"Looking back on it now, I was prepared for what I knew I was going to see. I just had no idea it would be Lorraine." She shook her head, the scene playing out in her mind like it was yesterday instead of a few weeks ago. Suzanne was on her knees, Lorraine fucking her from behind. They were obviously too busy to see her standing in the doorway.

Kelly retreated back down the hall and rummaged through Suzanne's purse. She pulled out her phone and key ring. As Suzanne screamed Lorraine's name, Kelly slid her house key off the ring and dropped it into her pocket. She erased her number from Suzanne's phone and did the same to Lorraine's, whose iPhone was on the coffee table next to a black lace bra she recognized as the one she gave Suzanne for her birthday a few months ago. The matching panties were on the floor by the couch.

"I didn't feel shock or anger. Just disgust."

She'd grabbed a beer from the fridge and sat down on the couch, then flipped through the channels until she found an old episode of Friends. *That was certainly apropos. One of them must have heard the TV and realized she was home, because shortly thereafter, Suzanne came out the bedroom tugging down her shirt and straightening her hair.*

"Hi, honey." *Suzanne's voice was sickly sweet.* "I didn't know you'd be home this early." *Her words ran together, her nervousness obvious. Kelly could tell she was trying not to look behind her to the bedroom. Kelly briefly wondered where Lorraine was hiding. Did she intend to sneak out after they'd left? Coward.*

"That's pretty obvious," *Kelly replied, her voice surprisingly calm. She watched as Suzanne's eyes flitted around the room as if checking for evidence. Her face paled when she found it. Her eyes were wide when they met hers.*

"I can explain," *Suzanne said.*

Kelly put her hand up to stop her. "No explanation necessary, Suzanne. I saw everything I needed to."

"But it's not what it looks like." *Suzanne's voice was almost pleading.*

"I don't think anyone would have any other interpretation of what was going on in my house and in my bed, and," *Kelly paused,* "with my best friend. Oh, wait." *Kelly hesitated again.* "With my ex-best friend."

"It's not her fault, Kel," *Lorraine said, coming out of the bedroom. Kelly wondered where she'd stashed her strap-on.*

"Don't blame Suzanne. It's my fault this happened."

Kelly laughed at the large red hickey on Lorraine's neck. She pointed to it.

"And somehow Suzanne had nothing to do with the hickey on your neck?" *Kelly asked, pretending skepticism.*

Lorraine's hand shot to her neck as she looked at Suzanne.

"Both of you get out of my house and my life. I don't want to hear from either of you ever again," *Kelly said, as calm as if she were saying where they were going to dinner. The calm was worse than any raving she could muster.*

"But," Suzanne and Lorraine said simultaneously, making Kelly laugh.

"You come together, and you even say the same words at the same time. How cute. Now you can leave together. Get out."

She turned up the volume and didn't look at either of them as they gathered their things and closed the front door behind them.

"So, tell me more about playing lacrosse," Matt asked.

Kelly was relieved she had changed the subject. She didn't want to dwell on what was.

"It keeps me young and makes me feel old at the same time."

"How so?" Matt asked.

"All the running helps keep me in shape, keeps the weight off. But the next day it takes a little longer to get out of bed and a few more minutes under the hot water in the shower." Kelly loved the game and would play until she wasn't able anymore.

"It's a pretty physical game, isn't it?"

"We're all padded up, but yes. With sticks flying everywhere and a hard little ball sailing through the air, you're bound to get a nick here and there."

"Is that how you got that?" Matt pointed to her cheek.

Kelly unconsciously reached up and touched her face. "No. I got that when one of my brothers threw a stick at me."

A warm smile filled Matt's face, and Kelly's heart skipped a little. It was doing that and more every time their eyes met.

"How many do you have?" Matt asked.

"Six."

Matt's eyebrows shot up. "Six?"

Kelly laughed. "That's typically people's reaction."

"Where are you in the birth order?"

"Guess." Kelly's flesh heated as Matt studied her.

"You're the baby."

"Yes, I am, and let me tell you that in and of itself is a challenge."

Matt imagined what it would be like for Kelly's dates to have to run the gauntlet of six brothers just to get her out the door.

"The story goes that my mom told my dad, 'You finally have your girl, and do not come near me with that thing again until you snip it.'" Kelly's eyes sparkled at the memory.

Matt winced. "That's a little TMI I'd never want to know about my own parents. Do you take after your mother?"

"That's the funny thing. I'm just like my father. I look like him, have the same mannerisms, same temperament, same cowlicks, and used to get into the same trouble, everything."

"And what does he think of that?"

"He wanted a little girl just like my mom. She laughs and points her finger at him and says, 'You asked for it.'" Kelly pointed her finger at Matt for emphasis.

"Sounds like you're close with your family."

"Yeah. I am. We live in about a twenty-minute radius of each other. We get together when we can, birthdays and anniversaries and stuff like that. My brothers are all married and have a pack of kids between them. My mother loves to say that only the best moms get to be called Grandma, so her life is complete."

"Any kids in your future?" Matt asked.

Kelly sensed something in her question but couldn't put her finger on what it was.

"I haven't thought too much about it. But I haven't ruled it out. I do know I don't want to do it alone. At least I don't think I do. It's got to be hard. Children take up every minute of your day when they're little, and suddenly they go from being totally dependent on you to asking you to shuttle them around to football and soccer practice and sleepovers. My sister-in-law says that she's nothing but an Uber driver."

"Tell me about your books," Kelly said, shifting the subject. "You said you're working on something sci-fi?"

"Yes. I was planning to do some writing on this trip, but I seem to be too busy."

Kelly heated at the fiery look in Matt's eyes.

"I can leave you alone. No." Kelly put her hands up before Matt could respond. "No. I can't leave you alone, so you're going to have to figure something out. You're mine for the next two weeks. If you want, of course."

Kelly watched Matt's eyes travel across her face, hesitate at her lips, then return to her eyes. She flushed all over at the sensuous act.

"I do."

Kelly's throat tightened at the thought of Matt saying those same words in a very different setting. Holy shit. Where had that come from? She needed to be very careful, but in the back of her mind she knew it was already too late.

"We'll have to go find a bookstore so I can pick up one of your books," Kelly said, needing to change the subject.

"I don't think there's a Barnes and Noble here."

"Then I'll go on Amazon and order it."

"I wouldn't spend your money on it," Matt replied.

"Why not? I thought all authors were always self-promoting. And besides. Now that I know you, I'm interested," Kelly added, hoping her previous statement didn't sound too harsh.

"Because they're geared to appeal to the nine-to-thirteen age groups."

"So, I'm a post-teen. I can still enjoy it. And speaking of enjoying it," Kelly said. "I really enjoyed *Tropical Nights*."

Kelly had googled Matt's pen name and was more than a little surprised when over a dozen books written by Alice Monroe appeared. She bought *Tropical Nights* and instantly downloaded it to her iPad. Eight pages in, Kelly thanked the eBook gods. She would have been turned on before she'd met Matt, but as she turned each page and touched herself, she imagined Matt's hands on her.

The expression on Matt's face when she clearly read between the lines and realized just how fulfilling Kelly had found it was priceless. It was a combination of shock and embarrassment.

"Why so surprised? It was good. I particularly liked the scene on the boat when Robbie..."

Matt put up her hands in surrender. "No need to go into details. I know what Robbie did."

"Have *you* ever done that?"

Matt blushed again. "Well," she said, her embarrassment turning to something much more interesting. "Sometimes authors write what they know."

Kelly was so aroused by the conversation she could probably come right here in the booth if the conversation continued.

"I bought all of them so, since your royalty check will be a bit larger next month, you can buy me another beer.

Matt laughed. "You're crazy."

"I've heard that before."

After lunch, they pedaled around the small downtown area, parking their bikes alongside others before going inside the stores. The shop owners were very welcoming and helpful, either due to their generous nature or the fact that they understood their livelihood depended on the tourist trade. Matt suspected it was the former, as a few were far less hospitable. The shops ranged from low-end tourist trinkets to high-end, locally designed jewelry. Matt was toying with the idea of buying the Tag Hauer watch the salesman had just fastened around her wrist.

"You have very good taste," Kelly said, coming up beside her. She'd wandered to the other end of the store while Matt looked at the watches in the locked display case.

"I have a confession to make," Matt said, trying to look serious.

"What?"

"I'm a watch whore."

"Excuse me?" Kelly asked, her brow furrowed in confusion.

"A watch whore. I love them. I have far too many, and I'm a sucker for one that conveys a certain image." The dozens of watches in her dresser were proof.

Kelly took several steps back, and Matt grew hot as Kelly's eyes traveled up and down her, paying particular attention to the hot spots in the middle.

"Buy it. It makes you look hot." She leaned into Matt and whispered, "Wear it, and nothing else, when you fuck me."

Matt's pulse raced, and her clit jumped in response to Kelly's sultry tone and her provocative command. "I'll take it. No need to wrap it."

The ride back to the hotel was painful, Kelly's clit hard in anticipation. She'd thought she'd had enough sex to be satisfied for a while, but the more time she spent with Matt, the more she wanted her. She needed to be careful, or she might end up falling for her. Kelly refused to let that happen. Suzanne, and many of her friends, had shown Kelly that the concept of exclusivity in a relationship was just that—a concept, and not reality. She wasn't going down that road again in the near future. Maybe even never.

By unspoken mutual consent, they quickly returned the bikes and practically ran to Kelly's room, making out like teenagers in the elevator during its awesomely slow trek to the sixth floor. After they dashed down the hall, they slammed the door shut behind them and began tearing off their clothes.

The bed had been neatly made, and Kelly wasted no time in tossing the covers onto the floor and pulling Matt with her on top of the crisp, white sheets.

"Jesus, I've wanted to fuck you all afternoon," Kelly declared just before taking one of Matt's nipples between her teeth and sliding her hand down Matt's stomach and into her. She was wet and ready. Matt moaned and tightened around Kelly's fingers. She flicked Matt's clit with her thumb.

"God, that feels good. I should have bought this watch my first day here." Matt gasped again and opened her legs wider.

"I don't know if I want to fuck you like this or with my tongue." Kelly mimicked her words with her fingers. She had never been this turned on, this fast, in her life. She was ready to come just by touching Matt.

"Those don't have to be mutually exclusive."

Matt's voice was harsh, coming in gasps, and Kelly knew, from the dozens of times before, that Matt was on the brink. She wanted to tease her, keep her poised on that cliff for as long as possible, bring her to the crest, then take her down, then back up again, but she was impatient to experience Matt's orgasm. She was exquisitely beautiful when she climaxed, and Kelly didn't want to waste time.

She impatiently slid down Matt's body, eager to reach her destination. Matt's breathing was fast and shallow, and Kelly easily slipped into that place that was already so familiar, so recognizable, so ready for her. With her tongue, she started to explore the places she knew made Matt writhe in pleasure.

"Ugh… God, that feels incredible." Matt gasped, her fingers in Kelly's hair. "Don't stop. Just like that."

"Now" was all Kelly needed to hear a few moments later, and she began to suck Matt's clit. Matt stiffened for just a moment as the flesh around her fingers pulsed, and then she came in a rush of pleasure so intense, Kelly followed an instant later. Matt held her close as wave after wave of orgasm shot through her. When Matt's shudders subsided, Kelly flicked her tongue over Matt's hard clit, causing another round to envelope her.

It was hours later and very dark when Kelly's stomach growled. She was lying on her side, her head on Matt's stomach. The sheets lay somewhere on the floor, the fan slowly circling overhead.

"I heard that."

Matt's voice rumbled in her ear as Kelly watched the smooth rise and fall of her breasts. She had been remembering what they tasted like, the way Matt's nipples grew hard under her fingers, in her mouth.

"You need to feed me if you expect me to keep this up." Kelly had barely gotten the words out when Matt sprang up and scrambled over the mussed sheets. She grabbed the phone and punched in a few numbers.

"Room service? This is room 6014."

They filled the time as they waited for dinner to arrive.

Long after the empty dishes were placed in the hall for pick-up by the kitchen crew, sensations flooded Kelly, and she felt the familiar pull of pending orgasm. She drifted away on memories of Matt's mouth and fingers dancing over her, her skilled hands tracing the lines and curves of her body and bringing it to life all over again. Sex had never been so good. Matt instinctively knew where to go and what to do once she got there. She wasn't shy about asking what Kelly wanted, often holding back until she told her.

Seconds after another blistering orgasm, Kelly had difficulty catching her breath. She gasped and tried to speak, her voice failing her. Instead, she reached for Matt, wrapped her arms around her, and fell into a deep sleep.

Kelly woke to the sun peeking through the curtains. She glanced at the clock, surprised to see it was after ten. Matt had left earlier, saying that if she didn't, she'd die of exhaustion. They'd made love for hours, and if she hadn't collapsed in sheer orgasmic exhaustion, they probably would still be at it. A rush of heat flowed through Kelly as she remembered how passionate Matt could be one minute and ravishing her the next. Matt was the most experienced, fun, intuitive lover she had ever had.

Those would be hard sheets to fill in the future, Kelly thought, and immediately a wave of emptiness rushed over her. She didn't want this to end. Didn't want to not experience Matt's laugh, her sense of humor, her touch. She bolted out of bed, her muscles protesting as she hopped into the shower. She could not and would not allow herself to think about Matt in that way. This was nothing but a vacation fling, and sex was always better on vacation. Kelly kept telling herself that as she tingled under the warm water.

CHAPTER TWENTY-TWO

Y ou going to get up, sleepyhead?"
"Leave her alone. She's been busy."
"And that's exactly why she needs to get up. I want details."

Voices pierced the darkness of sleep far too soon for Matt. She was physically and emotionally exhausted and needed rest. Good Lord. She hadn't had this much exercise in more years than she could remember. Maybe if she lay here pretending to be asleep, they'd leave her alone. Let her bask in her memories of being with Kelly. The bed bounced, and not in a good way.

"Get up," Sandra commanded, poking Matt. "It's almost noon, and we've been waiting forever to hear about it."

"What's with this 'we' business?" Becca piped up. "I'm minding my own business."

"Bullshit," Matt replied, rolling over onto her back. "When have you ever minded your own business?"

"Always. Just not when it comes to my best friends. Then it is definitely my business."

"All right. Let's hear it." Sandra settled in on the other side of Matt.

"Can I at least have some coffee before you two interrogate me?" Matt sat up, pulling the pillows against the headboard behind her.

Sandra handed her a large green mug, steam rising from the top. "The official name for this is quid pro quo." Sandra had her best lawyer voice going on. "I give you what you want, and you give us what we want in return."

Matt took several sips of her coffee. "I'm having fun, just as the court ordered," Matt said, referring to the edict her two friends had given her as one of the requirements of this trip.

"What kind of fun?"

"Adult fun."

"And?" Sandra asked when Matt didn't add anything to her statement.

"And didn't Becca already tell you this?" Matt replied, taking a sip of the hot coffee.

"Yes, but that was two days and nights ago. We want real-time data."

"I'm not going to kiss and tell. Been there, done that," she said, referencing her confession to Becca the other day.

"Well, you better start now because that mark on your neck is doing all the talking for you." Sandra pointed to the left side of her neck.

"Ran into a door," Matt answered sarcastically and tried not to squirm under their scrutiny.

"Looks more like a set of teeth to me," Becca added.

"You two are acting like this is high school," Matt said, grateful they couldn't see the other bite marks.

"So says the girl with a hickey on her neck."

"I do not have a hickey on my neck."

"Keep telling yourself that," Sandra said, laughing.

"You look like you got a little too much sun," Becca commented, pointing to her sunburned nose. "Too much time on your back?"

Both women laughed, and Matt couldn't help but join in. She loved her goofy, nosy friends, who had only her best interest at heart. Together they'd gone through good and bad, heartbreak and joy, and they'd always come out on the other side. This was no exception.

After getting cleaned up, they headed to the beach and miraculously found three vacant lounge chairs on the far side of the pool. They settled in and ordered tall, fruity, very strong alcoholic drinks and pizza. They chatted about people they've seen or met over the past few days and made up stories of what it would be like to live in a society of nothing but lesbians.

A few hours later, Matt's phone dinged, and she picked it up, expecting it to be Kelly because they'd made plans for dinner. She frowned when she recognized Cynthia's number.

"Something wrong?" Becca asked.

"It's Cynthia," Matt said, feeling like she had a bad taste in her mouth. Her mother-in-law always ruined her day. "Did I tell you the scene we had a couple of days before we left?" Both women shook their heads.

Cynthia had come over unannounced, undoubtedly because a car was parked in front of Matt's house, and it was only a little after eight. It belonged to a visitor she'd seen go into her neighbor's house when she had opened the curtains earlier in the morning.

"May I speak with you, Mattingly?"

Cynthia always used her formal name, even after the several times Matt had given her permission to shorten it. She doubted that Cynthia had ever been called anything but her full name in her life. She was petite and always put together to perfection. Andrea had never known exactly how old her mother was, and Matt guessed by now she'd be in her early sixties. Her skin was flawless, courtesy of Botox and expensive plastic surgery, her hair expertly colored to look natural. Matt had never seen a root of gray or a smudge of her lipstick. This morning was no exception.

"Of course, Cynthia. Come in."

The subtle scent of expensive perfume lingered in the air as her mother-in-law crossed the threshold.

"Would you like some coffee?" Matt asked out of politeness. The last thing she wanted to do was encourage the woman to make herself comfortable and stay a while. Matt chided herself when she remembered that Cynthia was never comfortable in her house, even when Andrea was still alive.

"No, thank you."

Matt led the way to the family room, and she could practically hear what was going through her mother-in-law's mind.

Andrea never would have allowed the baseboards to be chipped and dusty. Andrea never would leave a pile of Jordan's folded laundry on the table. She would have taken it upstairs and put it away. Andrea would have made Jordan put his sports bag in the hall closet where it belonged. Andrea never would have open, empty envelopes on the table, her bills exposed for anyone to see. Andrea never would have allowed spots on the patio door from the dog. Andrea never would have allowed a dog in the house, let alone a bed in the corner, toys strewn about. Andrea never would have...

"Have a seat." Matt pointed to one of the chairs across from the couch. Cynthia never sat on the couch, and Matt certainly didn't expect her to do so now. God forbid she sat on the place where debauchery and fornication had probably occurred on a daily basis. She always sat in one of the chairs, her back straight, and she always perched on the edge, ready to escape at any time. This time was no different. It was like she was afraid she'd catch something if she did.

When Andrea had told them she was pregnant, the look of shock and disgust that Cynthia, in all her perfectness, could not hide, said it all. What had Cynthia expected? She knew her daughter had been living with Matt for years, had brought her to family functions, introduced her as her partner, then her wife. Had she really thought they were just roommates? Two women sharing the bills?

She did come to the hospital when Jordan was born, appalled they had bestowed their son with Matt's father's name. She never volunteered to babysit, and Jordan had never spent the night at their house. But she refused to be called Grandma, or anything else that resembled it. Jordan called her GG, and Matt knew it made Cynthia nuts. What in God's name did she expect her grandson to call her? Mrs. Underwood? Matt knew that's how Cynthia probably thought he should address her. Her husband was somewhat better, but not much. It was clear who wore the pants in the family, controlled the purse strings, and every other cliché there was to describe their family dynamics.

Matt's parents, on the other hand, were completely accepting of their daughter's life. Her father helped her build the shed in the backyard, assemble the monster wooden swing set Jordan got for Christmas when he was five, and helped replumb the kitchen sink during a recent remodel. He beamed and handed out candy cigars when Jordan was born and held her up when Andrea was laid to rest. He doted on Jordan, and they often had "man time," where they would hang out at the park, see a stupid movie, or just generally do guy things. He taught Jordan how to pee in the woods and hold the door open for women of any age. He gave him the finer points of throwing a ball and being a good sport. He went to every event at his school and was often in the front row with the biggest camera. It wasn't anything Matt could not have done herself, but she encouraged Jordan to spend time with his grandpa. Her mother baked cookies and smothered him with kisses every chance she could. How grandparents could be so different was a mystery to Matt.

"What can I do for you, Cynthia?"

"Is Jordan here?"

This was her subtle way of finding out if Matt had shipped her son off to a friend's house for a sleepover so she could have an adult one.

"Yes. He's upstairs. Do you want me to call him down?" Matt doubted that was the reason she was here. She never asked to see her grandson.

"No. I came to speak with you."

Matt sat back on the couch and put her feet up on the coffee table. Cynthia practically blanched. Andrea never would have... *Matt waited for Cynthia to speak. She refused to make small talk. Cynthia never did small talk.*

"We know you're going to a place for homosexuals."

Cynthia had practically spat the word from her mouth like spoiled milk.

So that's what this is about, Matt thought. Another in a long line of unnatural acts that her daughter had to have been forced to endure because their daughter was not like that.

"The correct term is lesbian, Cynthia."

Matt watched Cynthia's expression turn sour, like she'd just tasted something unpleasant.

"We don't believe you are setting a good example for Jordan."

Not that Matt cared what the uptight woman thought, but she asked anyway, "How so?"

"Because of where you are going."

And what you're going to do there, *Matt knew Cynthia wanted to add, but the actions behind the words were unmentionable.*

"I'm going on a vacation, which, by the way, I have never had since Andrea died, with friends I knew before I met Andrea, who loved Andrea, and who stood beside me when she died. We're going to a safe place, with no civil war, gangs, drug lords, or human trafficking. It's a five-star resort that is not staffed with slave labor and has clean, running water and flush toilets. What's your point?"

"You are leaving Jordan to go and—"

"Jordan is going to a camp he has begged to go to for two years. One that I checked out and talked about with a lot of families that have sent their kids there. They have a spotless safety record and zero complaints. I am not leaving him just anywhere, as you're implying."

"I'm not implying—"

"Yes, Cynthia, you are. You are accusing me of leaving Andrea's child, my child, so I can go to the other side of the world and have sex with every woman on the island." Cynthia grew pale. *"Yes, Cynthia, don't kid yourself., That's exactly what you think I'm going to be doing. And it's in the British West Indies, not on the moon."*

Matt had never spoken to her mother-in-law like that, even though there were more times than she could count when she had wanted to. Andrea had been the buffer between them, and after her death, Matt had kept the peace for the sake of Jordan.

"I didn't...I wouldn't...I never..." Cynthia stuttered. It was the *first time Matt had ever seen her without something to say.*

"I think you should leave, Cynthia. This is my house, and I will not be insulted by you or anyone else about my parenting ability. I love Jordan, and ever since the day he was born, no, actually," Matt *hesitated for a second or two,* "ever since the day he was conceived, he has always been my number-one priority."

Matt stood and walked toward the front door. She opened it, her body language clearly signaling the conversation was over. As Cynthia approached, Matt said, "Andrea loved you very much, but she'd be ashamed of your behavior toward me and our son."

Cynthia glared at her as she walked past. "And don't come over without calling first. It's the polite thing to do." Matt used all her restraint not to slam the door behind her.

"Jesus, why don't you move?" Sandra asked when Matt finished retelling the unsettling event.

"Because she'd just buy the house across the street like she did that one. Did I ever tell you that their house was never really for sale when they bought it?" Both women shook their heads again. "They convinced the Moyers to sell. Made them an offer they couldn't refuse."

"What?" Becca asked, clearly incredulous.

"Joanne, whose son went to high school with the Moyers kids, lives around the corner. She was at the mailbox one day just a few months ago, and she told me that Cynthia and Harrison rang their doorbell and offered them cash."

"Andrea would wring their necks if she were alive." Sandra was spot on with her comment.

"If Andrea were alive, they wouldn't have to. They wouldn't have to worry about me disrespecting their daughter by continuing to live my life."

"That's just ridiculous," Becca said. "Do they expect you to stay single and celibate for the rest of your life?"

"Yes. They do."

"Well, one down, one to go," Sandra said.

Matt glanced at her watch. She had to head in and get cleaned up for her date with Kelly. Her voice mail pinged again, and she glanced at it to make sure it wasn't Jordan's camp calling. She'd return Cynthia's call tomorrow and put it out of her mind. "Speaking of the one that's down, I've got a date with Kelly for dinner. Don't wait up."

Chapter Twenty-three

Matt was chatting with Carol, the concierge on duty again that night, when Kelly came up the walk. She was wearing a yellow sundress that fell just above her knees, the spaghetti straps exposing her tan, well-defined arms and shoulders. Her hair was down, and something sparkled around her neck. When she saw Matt, she smiled and waved, the bracelets on her wrists jangling. If Matt had thought Kelly was sexy in a bikini, she was adorable in her dress. Matt had to swallow a few times before she could speak. She needed to be careful, or she'd get carried away and start having white-picket-fence thoughts. The idea stunned her. Where had that come from? Sure, they'd had several days of fun in the sun and the sheets, but when did it jump from fun to fences?

"Hi."

"Hi yourself."

"You…uhh…look nice." Matt had seen Kelly naked and had explored, up close and personal, every inch of her, and she still felt like an adolescent on her first date. Kelly smiled like she knew exactly what Matt was thinking.

"Thank you. You do too."

Matt was glad she'd taken the extra time to iron her shorts and shirt.

"Carol called us a taxi." Matt had to tear her eyes away from the hint of cleavage at the top of Kelly's scoop-neck dress. She was more than a little familiar with what was underneath, but it was enticing just the same.

A battered white Toyota 4Runner pulled into the circle and stopped under the portico. An elderly man in wrinkled, cut-off khakis two sizes too big and a T-shirt well beyond its prime hustled around the back of the vehicle and approached them.

"You two girls call for a taxi?"

Carol came around behind them and, with more than a little effort, yanked open the passenger door.

"Ladies," the driver said, his arm sweeping in a gesture indicating they should slide into the backseat.

"Maybe I should have read up a little bit more on the transit situation on the island before I came," Matt mumbled under her breath. The taxi they'd taken to dinner with Becca and Sandra had been nothing like this.

"That's on you," Kelly said, deadpan. "I was planning on being half naked on the beach or completely naked in my room with my girlfriend the entire time. I had no plans to get out and explore the city."

"I can help you with that," Matt said, winking at Kelly.

"Yes, you definitely can, but later. Right now, you need to feed me."

"Enjoy your evening, ladies." Carol slammed the door seconds after Matt pulled her leg inside.

The driver settled into his seat and turned the key. It took several tries before the vehicle sputtered to life.

"You are going to Mancuso's?" he asked over the rattle of the engine.

Matt met his eyes in the rearview mirror. "Yes, we are," she replied, forcing a smile and wondering what would die before they got to the restaurant—the vehicle or them.

"It's a very nice restaurant," the man commented. "Very good food. Very nice patio. Very romantic." He winked at Matt.

Kelly, sitting beside her, chuckled but kept a white-knuckle grip on the door handle.

They didn't have to worry about making conversation on the ride, because the driver went into endless detail about every bush, building, and tree along the route. As they drove Matt kept her eye on the terrain, wondering if it would be safer for them to walk back than have a similar return trip.

There were no seat belts, and Matt slid into Kelly on the sharp turn the driver had taken when pulling into the restaurant parking lot. Pebbles clanged as they hit the undercarriage. He pulled into a parking space, put the vehicle in park, and turned around.

"That will be US twenty dollars."

Matt tried to mask her surprise at the exorbitant amount for a trip she figured was less than three miles. She reached into her pocket and pulled out her cash, but Kelly touched her arm.

"I'll get it."

"No. I will. You can get the return trip." Matt handed the driver a twenty and a few ones and banged on the passenger door to get it open.

As soon as they were out of the vehicle, they both started laughing.

"You got the better end of the stick," Matt said. "If you think I'm going to get into that vehicle and ride back, you're nuts."

Kelly continued to laugh. "Well, if you think I'm going to walk all the way back to the resort on that road in these shoes, you're out of your mind."

Matt looked down at Kelly's shoes, but not before taking a long look at her bare legs.

"Because of that look in your eye, you'll need to buy me a drink first," Kelly said.

"My pleasure."

Matt's hand was warm on the small of her back as they walked through the restaurant and out onto the patio. The expression on Matt's face when she'd first seen her this evening had caused Kelly's stomach to flipflop, and with the roller coaster of the taxi, it still hadn't settled. If anything, the look on Matt's face had excited her even more than her touch.

She'd thought about Matt as she was getting ready for dinner— what her real story was and why she'd have friends who saw the need to send her here. Was it because her wife had died? That was years ago. Surely she couldn't still be grieving, could she? As attentive as

Matt was when they made love, the way their eyes locked when they came, the fact that she cried out her name and not someone else's told Kelly otherwise. Matt was obviously attracted to her. She knew it instinctively when Matt's eyes roamed over her and felt hot when they lingered on certain places.

She was right when she'd told Matt that it made her feel good that someone found her attractive. But she was also angry at herself for allowing Suzanne's actions to impact her self-esteem.

She'd looked at herself standing naked in front of the mirror in her hotel room earlier, seeing the effects of great sex. She was glowing, her breasts still full, nipples tender. She had red marks on her stomach where Matt had sucked her, teasing at first, then more passionately later. Other than the attention Matt had given her the past few days, Kelly thought she still didn't look half bad. The effects of time and gravity were evident, even at thirty-six, but she worked hard to not let them overtake her if she could help it.

Somewhere between finding Suzanne and Lorraine together and getting on the flight, Kelly had realized she really didn't care. Being with Suzanne had become more of a habit than a desire, and perhaps Suzanne had felt the same. However, that wasn't an excuse for her behavior. If Suzanne wanted out, she should have said so.

The waiter led them out onto the patio to a table with room for four but set for two. Matt held Kelly's chair as she sat down.

"Chivalry is not dead. Thank you."

Matt lightly trailed her fingers over Kelly's shoulders before she settled into the chair next to her. "Just being polite."

"Well, I appreciate it all the same."

"I am having dinner with a lady. And one that's quite beautiful. She deserves it."

A woman, who couldn't have been more than five feet tall if she were wearing thick socks and standing up real straight, took their drink order, recited the dinner specials, then left them alone.

"This looks exactly like the photos in the brochure Carol gave us," Kelly said, glancing around. The tables were covered in royal-blue tablecloths, accented with white linen napkins and flatware. In the center of each table a small candle burned, and occasionally

Kelly caught the scent of sandalwood. Thick shade sails, a little darker than the color of the cloudless sky, floated in the cool breeze, blocking out the late-afternoon sun.

Several boats were moored at the adjacent dock, three more jockeying for position as they approached. The waitress returned with their drinks and a basket of bread. She took their order and left as quickly as she had the first time.

Kelly raised her glass in a toast and waited until Matt did the same. "Here's to a lovely dinner. Thank you for the invitation."

"Here's to surviving the taxi ride to bring us to this lovely dinner." Matt touched her glass to Kelly's, a delicate "ping" filling the air.

Kelly sipped her drink, glad she had, because there was more Crown Royal than Coke in the short glass. She'd have to go easy on this cocktail, or she might end up doing something stupid—like fall for Matt. Heat flashed through Kelly, but she had enough sense to take several gulps of her water to cool her raging pulse. She wanted Matt again, and this was beginning to feel like more than a vacation fling. She hoped she didn't look as flushed as she felt.

They sat in comfortable silence until the waiter returned with steaming plates of their dinner. She came back a minute later and lit a can of Sterno, placing it at the edge of the table.

"This will keep the flies away," she explained. It also added five degrees to the table.

They made small talk about the scenery, the meal, and innocuous topics that people introduced over dinner as they were getting to know each other. Why were they even doing this? It wasn't like they would see each other after this. They had a week left, and then it would be over.

"Kelly?"

Matt's voice yanked Kelly back from the slippery slope she was falling into. She felt a burn low in her belly and a hard beat of her heart every time she thought of Matt. She was drawn to her, the air around them always electric. Matt brought out a side of her she didn't know existed. Erotic words accompanied with soft touches turned her body to fire. She didn't need Matt; she craved her.

"Are you all right? You seemed to go somewhere else for a minute." Matt reached over and touched her arm.

"Sorry. Yes, I'm fine," Kelly managed to say.

"You sure? You look a little flushed."

"Because I keep remembering how magical your tongue is." Might as well go with the truth, she thought.

Matt looked around. "Waiter," she called, holding her arm in the air to signal her. "Check, please."

Chapter Twenty-four

The trip back to the hotel was the opposite of their white-knuckle ride to the restaurant. The driver was a neatly dressed young man driving a sparkling clean Chevy Impala in immaculate condition. He followed the speed limit, took corners at an appropriate speed, and didn't dominate the conversation. As a matter fact, he didn't speak at all, and Matt added a generous tip when he dropped them off.

"How was your dinner, ladies?" Carol asked, coming around the concierge's desk.

"It was lovely, just as you recommended," Kelly said.

Matt couldn't remember the last time someone had used the word lovely in a sentence. It was sweet. Kelly was warm, charming, witty, and absolutely beautiful. Matt had almost mentioned Jordan during dinner, but she saw no point. After she got on the plane to go home, she'd never see Kelly again. It wasn't like she was going to be his stepmother.

Kelly took her hand as they walked through the lush landscape to her room. They passed several couples out for a stroll, the sound of wet flip-flops striking the cement as they passed. They didn't rush quite as much to get back to Kelly's room as they had yesterday afternoon, but they still hurried, eager to continue where they'd left off that morning.

Once inside, their eyes locked as Kelly led them to the bedroom. The maid had been in for the turndown service, leaving a small mint on the pillow. Matt lowered Kelly onto the crisp sheets and kissed her. Slowly, this time, they undressed each other, Matt taking her time revealing the warm, smooth skin she knew was underneath. She lifted Kelly's dress over her head. She wasn't wearing a bra, and Matt's breath caught in her throat. Kelly's nipples were hard, begging for attention.

Her lips skimmed over one, then the other, and then traced a pattern from the top of Kelly's legs to the bottom of her feet, gently tickling her toes. Her hands joined the trip back and settled on the wet triangle between Kelly's thighs, the last barrier to her pleasure. She slowly removed the silk panties and leaned back on her heels to regard Kelly in awe.

"You are so beautiful," she managed to say. No way could those few words convey the wonder and amazement of seeing Kelly bared so boldly for her.

"Take off your clothes," Kelly ordered her. "I need to feel all of you."

Matt stood and pulled off her shirt and removed her shorts, her eyes never leaving Kelly's. When she was completely naked, Kelly reached for her, drawing her down so her body completely covered hers.

Matt sighed with pleasure. She wanted to go slowly, to prolong the sensations as long as she could and make this as wonderful for Kelly as it was for her. Kelly's fingers were in her hair.

"You feel so good," Kelly said.

Matt gently caressed Kelly's cheek with the back of her fingers. She kissed her again. Moving lower, she took one of Kelly's breasts into her mouth and gently bit the nipple. Kelly whispered her name and moved under her, increasing their connection. Matt slid her hand to Kelly's stomach, across her hips, caressing ever so closer to the warmth awaiting her. She teased the inside of Kelly's thighs and came agonizingly close to her clitoris, waiting to be invited. Kelly raised her hips, and Matt stilled her hand and looked into her eyes.

The fire in Kelly's eyes was blazing and left no doubt as to her desire. Kelly slid her hand down Matt's arm and placed it over Matt's. She moved it to her clitoris.

"Oh, God, please touch me."

At the first brush of contact, Kelly closed her eyes, arched her back, and moaned with pleasure.

"God. You are so beautiful." Matt watched her fingers move over Kelly's warm, moist center. Kelly began to writhe rhythmically beneath her, and Matt's own desire skyrocketed.

Touching Kelly was almost more than she could bear, and she forced back her own climax to watch Kelly. Riding a feeling of euphoria that she had never imagined, she watched Kelly's hand on hers as they brought her to orgasm. Matt continued to stroke her as the spasms peaked a second time.

Kelly shifted, and in an instant her hand found Matt's rock-hard clit. She buried her face in Kelly's neck as she immediately climaxed into Kelly's hand. Lights flashed behind her eyes, and she forgot to breathe as shudder after shudder racked her body.

Matt got her breathing under control and raised her head and looked at the woman she'd just made love to. Kelly was the most beautiful woman she'd ever seen. A sheet of sweat covered her neck and drew Matt's lips once again. As she kissed and licked the sensitive skin, she began to stroke Kelly again. She immediately lifted her hips in response.

"I don't think I can do that again," Kelly said, but her body was telling a very different story.

"Then let's do this." Matt quickly shifted and replaced her hand with her tongue.

"Oh, God, Matt."

Matt slowed her tongue, tasting the juices that flowed freely. Breathing heavily, Kelly gasped each time her tongue lightly slipped over her clitoris.

"Now."

It was the only word Matt needed to hear as she applied just enough pressure for Kelly to come again.

Matt took Kelly in her arms, cradling her as the aftershocks of her orgasm left her sated. She reached down and pulled the sheet up to cover them both.

CHAPTER TWENTY-FIVE

A nd this is your throttle. It's what gives the machine gas."
Matt looked at Kelly and rolled her eyes at the man's
condescending tone. She had a scathing comeback on the tip of her
tongue, but one look from Kelly made her keep her mouth shut. It
had been only four days since they'd met, but Matt thought it felt
like much, much longer.

"Two hours, right?" Kelly asked, confirming the amount of
time they'd reserved the Waverunner for.

"Yes, and we charge by the minute if you're late," he said, as if
they couldn't tell time.

They zipped up their life jackets, and Kelly climbed on behind
Matt.

"And another thing," he said, practically leering at Kelly. Only
her legs were visible, the bulky vest covering the upper half of her
body. Her hair was in a ponytail out the back of an Atlanta Braves
baseball cap, and her dark sunglasses hid her eyes.

"We have GPS trackers, so if you girls get lost, we'll be able
to find you."

"Don't worry." Matt slid her sunglasses down her nose so the
man could see her eyes.

"We know exactly where we're going and what we're going to
do when we get there." She winked at him just before she squeezed
the throttle, leaving him and his shocked expression in her wake.

They were on a white-and-lime-green Yamaha VX Deluxe
Waverunner that rocketed them from zero to forty miles an hour,

and in less than a minute, they were in open water. It was choppier than the calm water of the inlet, the ocean waves splashing water in Matt's eyes. After a few similar drenches, her eyes burned from the salt and she released her grip, the big machine slowing to a stop.

"I can't see anything," Matt said as a wave lifted the ski, then set it back down for another wave to do the same. "This salt water's burning my eyes."

"Me too," Kelly said from behind her. She opened the hatch behind her seat and pulled out her blue backpack. After rummaging around, she handed Matt a bottle of water.

"Here," she said. "Rinse out your eyes."

The cold water was shocking when it hit her face. She tipped her head back and flushed her eyes. "Shit, that's cold, but it feels good." She handed the flask back to Kelly, who made her own sounds of relief.

"Let's put on the goggles we brought," Kelly said, reaching into their bag. "That should help."

They had brought along snorkeling gear, intending to view the coral up close and personal once they reached the island in the distance.

"How do I look?" Matt asked after donning her mask. It was neon yellow. "Shit," she exclaimed, grabbing the handlebars of the ski as a wave threatened to topple them. They both laughed.

"As good as I probably do, but I don't care. Let's go," she said. "I have plans for you when we get there." She pointed to the island.

Kelly leaned in and kissed her, their clunky goggles banging against each other. She tasted like salt, warm, summer sun, and promise.

"Hang on," Matt said before squeezing the throttle to the max.

The water was crystal clear as they approached the shoreline. A stingray lazily swam around them, its large fins making it look like it was flying through the water, its barbed tail at least three feet long. Matt glanced at her watch, conscious of the time they needed to be back. It had taken them ten minutes to reach the island after stopping to check out an old, rusted cargo ship that had run aground during a storm a dozen years earlier.

Matt pulled out a rope she found in the cargo hold and tied one end to the handlebars of the ski. The other she wrapped around the trunk of a sturdy tree not far from the shoreline. She double-checked that the rope was securely fastened.

"As much as I'd love to be stranded on a deserted island with you, I really don't want to be stranded on a deserted island," Matt said. She held out her hand. "Come on. Let's take a walk."

The sand was soft and warm as they strolled down the shoreline holding hands. The sun was high in the sky when Matt pulled Kelly under a large tree, the canopy of leaves shading them from the hot, midday sun. She spread out the large beach towel they'd brought with them and sat down, pulling Kelly with her.

Matt turned to Kelly, all kinds of fun, naughty things dancing through her imagination.

"You were saying something about what you wanted to do with me when we got here."

Desire flared in Kelly's eyes, and Matt's clit began to twitch in anticipation. She'd never made love outdoors—in a tent during a long, rainy afternoon didn't count. The image of their naked bodies worshipping each other in the sun was heady. No, it was downright hot—no pun intended.

Kelly reached behind her back and untied the string that secured her bikini top around her chest. The material shifted, giving Matt more than a little peek at her breasts. She was reaching around her neck when Matt stopped her.

"Let me."

Kelly dropped her hands into her lap, and Matt slowly untied the string that held the two small triangles over her breasts. Even though she'd seen, touched, and tasted Kelly's breasts dozens of times, the anticipation of seeing them bare before her again was exciting.

"Every time I see you, I want you," Matt whispered, her voice husky with desire as she let the top slide from Kelly's breasts.

Kelly's breasts weren't perfect. One was a little larger than the other, and she wasn't a teenager anymore, but they were perfect to Matt. Her hand shook as she traced the outline of one, then the other, each circle getting smaller on her path to an erect nipple.

Kelly's breathing was quick and shallow, and Matt had barely touched her. The ability to excite her with the whisper of a finger was heady. Kelly shifted, allowing Matt to slide her shorts over her enticing hips and down her long legs. She lay back, naked, as Matt looked at her.

"You are so beautiful," Matt said, the words not even beginning to describe the sight in front of her. She ran her fingertip down the center of Kelly's chest, making lazy trails across her stomach, teasing just above her pubic bone. Kelly's hips lifted in obvious anticipation. Her eyes were closed, allowing Matt complete access to her, and she was overwhelmed with desire to please her, have her, possess her. Kelly parted her legs.

"Touch me." Kelly's words were part command, part plea, and Matt's head spun.

Still using just one finger, Matt slid inside warm, wet folds, flicking over Kelly's hard clit. Kelly grabbed a handful of towel and sand. Her knees rose and dropped open, giving Matt greater access. Her skin was flushed, her breathing ragged as she offered herself completely to Matt. The trust at this moment was overwhelming, and Matt felt it to her core.

Emotions Matt had never experienced swirled around her. Making love in the dark of night or the light of day was no match to the connection she felt as she made love to Kelly under the eyes of nature. Matt wanted her tongue to mirror the same exciting trail as her finger had—lick the salt, sweat, and desire from Kelly's skin. She wanted to slide her tongue inside her warm, wet center until she screamed her name as she came. But this scene, before her right now, could not be bested by anything she could imagine.

Kelly opened her eyes and locked her gaze with hers. They were ablaze with desire, filled with trust, and glazed with need.

"Make me come."

Matt watched Kelly transform into the most beautiful, captivating, mesmerizing woman she had ever seen as she crested the peak of orgasm.

"Oh my God, what you do to me," Kelly said, her head starting to clear and her pulse slow to an almost normal rate. She'd thought she'd had the best orgasms of her life with Matt, but this one was indescribable. If she had died the instant it hit, she would die a very happy woman.

It wasn't Matt's skill, though she definitely knew what she was doing and exactly what Kelly needed, that set her apart from all the others. It was the intensity of her touch, the way she made Kelly feel like she was the first and only woman she'd ever made love to.

It didn't take more than Matt's eyes on her to make her come. One touch, or one hundred, was all she needed for her body to explode into a million pieces scattered across the universe. And the way Matt held her afterward brought them all back together again. Kelly had had mind-blowing orgasms before, but nothing compared to how she felt when Matt touched her, put her mouth on her, whispered in her ear, "Come for me."

Kelly opened her eyes, the blue sky across the horizon cloudless. She lay curled against Matt's side, Matt's arms around her. She must have fallen asleep right after, because Matt was still fully clothed. A surge of desire drove her to action.

"Mmm," Matt murmured as Kelly unsnapped her shorts and slid her hand inside. Matt was wet and shifted just enough to give Kelly better access.

"We're gonna be late if you keep that up," Matt said, not making a move to stop her.

"My credit card has an unlimited max," Kelly said, pulling Matt's shorts off and settling between her legs.

"Hot and rich," Matt hissed when Kelly parted her warm lips. "I'm yours for the taking."

Kelly's heart hammered as she exposed Matt's center like she'd never seen it before. Her tongue explored familiar territory, yet new and exciting at the same time. They'd made love more times than she could count, each as glorious and thrilling as the first. Was this how it was supposed to be? The same act, with the same body parts, was unique every time? How could that be? God knew what she was doing when she blessed women loving women.

"God, Kelly, you make me feel so incredibly alive," Matt said, moving restlessly, sounding hoarse. "I don't care how you do it. Just don't stop."

Matt tensed, and Kelly knew she was a heartbeat away from orgasm. Kelly finally understood the phrase "one with nature." An instant later Matt let out a long, pleasure-filled moan, but not before saying, "Don't ever stop."

"That's $241.77 added to your bill for late charges," the man said, looking at Matt, then Kelly. She knew what he was thinking, and she was more than happy to give it to him.

She kissed Matt on the lips, surprising her. "And worth every penny."

The man's mouth dropped open, and Kelly took Matt's hand as they walked to the waiting taxi.

CHAPTER TWENTY-SIX

They were in a taxi returning from dinner the next night when Kelly said, "I have reservations for deep-sea fishing tomorrow. Interested?"

"I've never been," Matt replied, images of the *Deadliest Catch* series flashing through her mind.

"I have, and it's a lot of fun. You ride around in a boat, catch some sun, snag a few fish, and drink beer," Kelly said. "How is that not fun? Unless you have something against fishing?" She looked worried.

"No, no, not at all," Matt said, trying to reassure her. It did sound like fun, especially the part that entailed spending the day with Kelly. "What do I bring?"

"We have to get a fishing license, but we can get that at the dock before we board. You don't need to worry about bringing cash for anything. My treat," Kelly said, her smile dazzling. "Bring a backpack and some sunscreen, SPF 30 at least. We'll be on the water most of the day, and your face and neck and, especially with your short hair, the tops of your ears will get fried, if you're not careful. Better bring a hat if you have one. And don't forget sunglasses. The glare off the water is brutal."

"You sound like a real expert," Matt said jokingly. It was obvious Kelly had done this a few times and was excited to go again.

"And don't forget a towel and some Dramamine if you're prone to seasickness. Dress in layers. It might be cool on the water but will get warm once the sun comes up."

"The sun comes up?" Matt asked, not liking the sound of that phrase. She was so not a morning person. "What time do we need to leave?"

"We need to be at the dock at five thirty."

"As in five thirty in the morning?" When Kelly nodded, she asked, "Is there such a thing as sunset fishing?" she asked hopefully, even though she knew better.

"That's called a dinner cruise, silly," Kelly said, her laughter filling the small car. She pecked her on the cheek. "That's the day after tomorrow."

Two men were waiting at slip 68 when Matt and Kelly approached the next morning. Matt had had two cups of coffee, and Kelly had insisted she eat a light breakfast before they left her room. She'd gone directly to her suite after the taxi had dropped them off to get what she needed for their outing the next day. Becca was sitting on the balcony, a glass of wine in her hand when she walked in.

"How was dinner?" she asked, indicating for Matt to sit in the chair next to her.

"It was good. Some Mexican restaurant, but I don't remember the name of it. It had round sandstones in the shape of sand dollars on the floor. Kind of cool."

"How was the food?"

"Okay, but nothing to write home about. The margaritas were okay too. I think the chips were the best thing the place had going for it."

"Things seem to be going pretty good for you two. Not that we're complaining, but we haven't seen much of you."

"We're having fun," Matt replied. "Isn't that what I was supposed to do? Have fun?"

"And get laid," Becca interjected. "And by the blush on your cheeks, I think that's going more than just okay."

"You could say that." In her own mind Matt would categorize it as magnificent, mind-blowing, earth-moving, and a variety of other adjectives she could name.

"I'm sorry I haven't been around much. We're supposed to go fishing tomorrow, but I'll cancel and spend the day with you two."

"You'll do no such thing," Becca said. *"Get whatever you need for tomorrow and get out of here. I know you want to. If I had a gorgeous woman look at me like she wanted me for breakfast, lunch, dinner, and dessert, I wouldn't be hanging around with my friends. Go,"* Becca said, using her hand to shoo her away. *"Go and have fun. That's what you came here for."*

❖

They boarded the boat after signing the manifest and introducing themselves to the captain. They paid a couple of dollars for a bag for their fish, the deckhand telling them it was bad luck not to get one.

"Do you ladies want to enter the jackpot?" the young deckhand asked.

"What's the game?" Kelly asked.

"Actually, we have several, and they're all easy. The first is for the person who catches the first fish of the day, the second is for who catches the biggest, and of course we have the upchuck."

"The upchuck?" Matt asked, her stomach already having an idea of what that game was.

"The first person to upchuck, of course." The man laughed and Kelly joined him.

"How much in the pot?" Kelly asked.

"Twenty dollars each game."

"We're in," she said, pulling her wallet out of the satchel and handing the man six twenty-dollar bills.

"You didn't have to pay for me," Matt said after the man scampered away in the direction of the other passengers.

"I said this day is my treat, and I meant it. Let's get settled," she said, pointing toward a pair of deck chairs. "I'm sure the captain will give us the safety briefing and what to expect for the day." Kelly was right, and after the captain's briefing, they headed out of the bay and into the open water.

The deckhands spent the forty-five minutes it took to get them to the fishing spot setting up the gear and giving instructions to the first timers. Matt paid close attention, not wanting to mess up in front of Kelly.

The boat slowed, and the deckhands dropped an anchor in the front and one in the rear of the boat. Matt stood.

"Hang on a minute," Kelly said, her hand on Matt's arm. "They need to get settled first, and we don't want to get in their way."

When the captain finally gave the all clear, Kelly headed to the bait station and returned a minute later with a small bucket.

"What is that?" Matt asked. It didn't look like anything she'd ever seen. It had an elongated body, very large eyes, and what looked like a bunch of tentacles coming out of its mouth. It was downright ugly.

"Squid," Kelly said, reaching into the bucket and handing one to her. Matt must have hesitated a second too long, because Kelly said, "I'll bait your hook for you."

"No. that's okay," Matt replied. "I can bait my own hook. I just don't know what to do with it. I'll watch you first, then do it."

"With squid, you don't need to change your bait unless the fish take it. But hopefully when they do, they'll take the hook with it, and you've got one." Kelly's eyes lit up, a sure sign she was eager to get going on the day's adventure.

Kelly won the jackpot for the first fish of the day, which weighed in at a little over seventeen pounds. As she was taking it off the hook, the captain told Kelly what it was, but Matt couldn't hear because she was in the process of winning the upchuck jackpot. Several humiliating minutes later, the contents of Matt's stomach were fish bait. One of the deckhands teased her that since it was her "bait," she'd catch the biggest fish of the day. He was right, and by two thirty they were on their way back to shore.

"I'm exhausted," Matt said as they waited for their taxi. Her arms were still quivering from the exertion of reeling in her twenty-eight-pound snapper.

"I know," Kelly said. "It wears you out."

"It was a lot of fun." Since they were on vacation, they'd released any fish they caught so they didn't need to worry about what to do with their catch.

"Even when you barfed your breakfast?" Kelly teased good-naturedly.

Kelly had kept a close watch on Matt for the remainder of the expedition, and instead of being embarrassed by the entire event, she felt comforted knowing someone was watching out for her.

"Especially *after* I barfed my breakfast." It was true. She had felt much better on an empty stomach.

Kelly yawned. "I need a nap."

"I like that idea," Matt said, her energy suddenly increasing at the thought of Kelly naked in bed.

"Oh, no, missy. Don't get that look in your eyes. I stink like fish, and I have squid guts all over me, plus eight coats of sunscreen."

"I don't know what look you're talking about," Matt said, feigning innocence. "I think you're sexy as hell with that deadliest-fisherwoman's aura about you."

"You think I'm sexy? Like this?" Kelly indicated her clothes.

Matt faced her and stepped close, their breasts almost touching. Kelly's eyes darkened with the familiar look of arousal, and Matt knew she would never grow tired of it.

"I think you're sexy all the time." Kelly swallowed hard, her eyes darkening even more. Matt leaned in and whispered in her ear. "Especially when you smell like squid and fish guts."

Kelly burst out laughing and pushed Matt away with both hands on her chest. "You are such a bullshitter."

Kelly was still chuckling as the taxi pulled up. They slid into the backseat, and Matt was quiet, lost in her thoughts. She wasn't bullshitting. She saw Kelly as beautiful, exciting, sensual, and sexy as hell every minute she was with her, and that thought scared the hell out of her.

CHAPTER TWENTY-SEVEN

Several days later, after lazy morning sex and a late breakfast, Kelly called for a taxi from the front desk. They rode to a small dock, where she had reserved a catamaran for the afternoon. When she paid for this trip the plan had been that she and Suzanne would sail around the island, but spending the afternoon with Matt was going to be so much better. After a few brief instructions, the deckhand pushed them away from the dock.

The sun was warm, and they were the only ones on the water. They sailed for about an hour, and as Matt dropped the anchor, Kelly slipped off her top. She liked the way Matt's eyes burned over her from behind her sunglasses.

"So, about that thing Robbie did in Chapter Eight in *Tropical Nights*," Kelly stated, stepping out of her bikini bottoms and tossing them to the side. She heated at the anticipation as Matt scrambled out of her clothes and walked toward her.

Several hours later they sailed back into the dock, tired, thirsty, and a little sunburned in places that normally didn't see much of the sun, if any. They were thirty minutes late, and Kelly tipped the teenager generously.

They went into town and stopped at the Skull Rock Cantina. It was blistering hot in the late afternoon, and the restaurant had no air-conditioning but plenty of large oscillating fans. The place had a lot of character, a large skeleton dressed in surf shorts and a brightly colored flowered shirt greeting them by the front entrance.

A large sombrero was on his head, a plastic margarita glass in his bony hands.

"Isn't that style of skeleton called something?" Kelly asked.

"It's a calaca, the Spanish name for skeleton. It's traditionally decorated for the Mexican Day of the Dead festival."

Kelly's fingers flew over her keyboard on her phone. "According to Wikipedia, calacas are generally depicted as joyous rather than mournful figures," she said, shading her screen from the glare of the sun. "They are often shown wearing festive clothing, dancing, and playing musical instruments to indicate a happy afterlife. This draws on the Mexican belief that no dead soul likes to be thought of sadly, and that death should be a joyous occasion."

"I'm not so sure about that," Matt said, as a brief wave of sadness drifted over her face, then was gone. "They are really colorful and fun, if a skeleton can even be called fun."

The theme carried through the restaurant, with photos and knick-knacks of calacas on the tables. The walls were painted bright yellows and green, with colorful pillows in the booths. The restaurant was charming, and Kelly made a note to stop at the small gift shop by the front door. Her accountant would love something from here. They found an empty booth and collapsed in it.

"I am exhausted," Matt said, raising her beer to her lips.

Kelly's heart skipped. Jeez, even Matt simply drinking beer made Kelly want to strip her and kiss every hot, sweaty inch again. She had it bad and needed to rein it in.

"But in a good way." Matt winked at her, and Kelly's clit throbbed. "A very good way."

"Well, a few more days, and you can go home and get some rest."

A flash of something passed over Matt's suddenly serious face, then just as quickly disappeared.

"Isn't that always the way it is with vacations?" Kelly said quickly, noticing the subtle shift in Matt. "You work your ass off to get ready, then work even harder to catch up after you get back." She saw Matt relax a little and doubted she was even aware of her reaction.

"I've got a pretty good crew, and the work doesn't stop when I'm gone, so that's not the problem. It's the paperwork that's probably stacked a foot high that I'll have to plow through." Kelly sensed that Matt didn't want to talk about anything serious. And what would they even talk about that was serious? The biggest thing on her mind was what time her flight left in a few days.

"I saw a tattoo parlor upstairs when we came in. I'd like to stop by and see what they have."

While exploring Matt's body in the boat, Kelly had asked about each of her tattoos and where she'd gotten them. Each one had a story behind it, and Kelly learned a little more about Matt with every one. One was a drawing a child had made of two stick figures holding hands, a sun overhead. One depicted a young boy, the other a woman with long hair, and they were holding hands. When she'd asked Matt about it, she'd been evasive as to who, if anyone, it was. That had troubled Kelly, but she pushed it out of her mind. It wasn't her place to force Matt to tell her, even if she could. Obviously, it meant something to her that she didn't want to share.

"Looking for anything special?" Kelly asked when the waiter brought a basket of warm chips and salsa to their table.

"I don't know. Maybe something with waves, something related to this trip. I'll have to see if anything strikes my fancy."

"You strike more than my fancy," Kelly said before she had a chance to stop and think about what her words might mean. This was not good. She held her breath for Matt's reaction.

Matt's left eyebrow slowly rose, and she smiled, the same expression that was a prelude to mischief. She was beginning to read Matt pretty well.

"You don't say." Matt smiled wickedly. "I never would have guessed. Here all this time I thought you tolerated me because you were too polite to tell me to get lost."

"I'd never tell you to get lost." Shit, thought Kelly. Another faux pax. She needed to get her raging hormones under control, and fast, before she declared her undying love for Matt.

Undying love? What the fuck! Matt was looking at her so intently, a lone bead of sweat slid down her sunburned back. Had she done it now? Had she stepped in something neither one really wanted or could do anything about even if they wanted to? She'd definitely had too much sun. She wanted to take back the last few minutes of her life.

Matt was studying her, and Kelly had no idea what was going on behind her blue eyes. Over the past several days she'd learned what each different expression meant. There was the twinkle that said she was in a mischievous mood, sadness and darkness that she never shared, peacefulness when they were anywhere near water, anxiety that Kelly had only seen once or twice the first day they met, and desire, which came just before she reached for her. But this was different. It was a cross between contemplation and debate. The longer Matt looked at her, the more uncomfortable Kelly became. An overwhelming feeling that this was a defining moment hovered over her. Finally, Matt spoke.

"Ditto."

After three beers each, two bowls of chips, and sharing a huge order of nachos, they climbed the stairs to the tattoo parlor. Matt had googled the place while they ate and had been impressed with the artist, the sole proprietor of the shop.

"There's a lot to consider when getting a tattoo," Matt had explained after Kelly asked.

"Like what?"

"Obviously the talent of the artist. Ink is forever, and if the tattooist doesn't have a steady hand or a creative eye, you're stuck with it the rest of your life."

"Can't you get it covered with something else?'

"Sure, but even that can be problematic if not done right."

"That's too much pressure for me," Kelly said.

The bell above the door rang, and they stepped inside, Matt leading the way. The room was small, maybe thirty feet square, with mirrors on one wall, a desk and printer in the corner, and a coffee table in front of several chairs.

A thin woman in her mid-thirties was bent over the leg of a well-muscled man lying on a table wrapped in some sort of protective covering. She held the tattoo gun in her gloved left hand, her long hair in a messy bun on top of her head. Both arms were covered in intricate designs, and Kelly wondered if she'd done them herself or if there was such a thing as professional courtesy. "I'll be with you in a minute," she said, not looking up.

"No problem. I'll just look around," Matt replied, picking up one of the three-ring binders on the table.

They sat next to each other on a small couch, their arms and legs touching. Kelly's pulse began to pick up, as it always did when she felt Matt's skin. She shifted, creating some space between them.

While Matt thumbed through the book, Kelly looked around as the buzz of the tattoo needle filled the silence. On the walls were the traditional half-naked women, cartoon characters, birds, flowers, animals, and various mythical creatures. The place was spotless and smelled slightly like disinfectant.

"What are you looking for?" Kelly asked as Matt flipped the pages. Each design was either a sketch or photo of the actual tattoo and protected from dozens of hands and fingers by clear, heavy-duty sheet protectors.

"I'm getting a feel for her work—the intricacy, the attention to detail, the creative aspect, that sort of thing."

Matt was bent over the book, obviously concentrating as her eyes moved over each page. Her fingers traced the image, and Kelly flashed to all the times they'd traced her. A flush of heat passed through her.

"What can I do for you?" the woman asked, pulling off her plastic gloves and walking toward them. The man was checking on the progress of his new ink. She held out her hand and Matt took it. "I'm Sophia."

"Matt, and this is Kelly. Nice to meet you. What can you do with this?" Matt asked, taking a folded piece of paper from her back pocket.

Kelly studied it upside down while the woman looked at it. It was a drawing of a camping scene, complete with a trailer, trees, and a fire pit.

"Where were you thinking?" she asked, eyeing Matt's bare arms and legs with more than professional inquiry.

Jealousy flared, and Kelly started to see green around the edges. Whoa! Stop that right now, she thought. She had no claims on Matt, even for the next few days. She didn't hear their conversation; she was trying to get her own thoughts back in the right place. That was a laugh, because ever since Matt had boarded the plane, her thoughts had been out of place.

"Okay, thanks." Matt extended her hand. "I don't leave for a few days. I may be back."

The woman took it. "Please do," she said, holding Matt's hand far too long. "I'm here till ten every evening."

Kelly had to concentrate not to stomp down the stairs. The gall of the woman to come on to Matt like that. Didn't she have any professional scruples? You don't hit on customers. Or maybe she did. Mose who came to her shop were probably just like Matt, on vacation and here one day and gone the next. What a great gig for hooking up.

"You okay?" Matt asked when their feet were back on solid ground.

"Sure," Kelly lied. She knew she wasn't convincing when Matt took her arm and stopped her. Kelly forced herself to calm down and look at Matt. The last thing she needed was for Matt to see rage in her eyes. She decided to take the offense.

"Did you not want to get it?" she asked, referencing the drawing Matt had shown the woman.

"No. She was crazy expensive, but that's not what I meant."

"Do you want to try somewhere else? I'm sure there are other places on the island." Kelly knew she was probably blabbering, but the intense look she was getting from Matt was making her nervous.

Matt pinned her with her look, hard, her eyebrows furrowed for a few more moments, then said, "No. I'm good."

Chapter Twenty-eight

What was all that about? Matt wondered as they walked through the parking lot and out onto the sidewalk. Was Kelly jealous? Matt wasn't that much out of practice not to recognize that Sophia was definitely interested in more than business. She'd held her hand just a bit longer than was professionally appropriate, and her eyes had wandered lazily over her body in more than a professional way. She, however, was not interested. Kelly was all Matt wanted, and no other woman moved her at all. Kelly had her complete attention. Didn't she know that?

Kelly was distant as they strolled through the shops, Kelly picking up a trinket or two for her employees. Conversation was stilted and forced, and Kelly was obviously doing her best to hide it.

"I'm ready to head back whenever you are," Kelly said after pocketing her change from the friendly clerk behind the counter.

"Sure. I'll get us a taxi." Matt wasn't sure what else to say. The mood had certainly shifted, and she wasn't entirely sure why.

They rode the five minutes back to the hotel in silence, the tension between them thick. It had been a long time since Matt had had to figure out what a woman was thinking, and she was definitely rusty.

"Will I see you later?" They hadn't made any plans for the evening, Matt assuming they'd grab a bite at the restaurant.

"If you want to. I don't want to monopolize your time."

Kelly's answer took Matt aback. *If I want to? Monopolize my time? What the hell?* "Of course, I want to. That is, if you do." The conversation was the oddest they'd ever had. What was next? I like you. Do you like me?

"Sure. How about we meet in the dining room in an hour. I need to freshen up a bit."

"Okay," Matt said. "I'll see you then, I guess."

She watched Kelly disappear around the corner, and Matt shook her head as she walked toward her room. She took a detour and headed to the water, needing a few minutes of the rambling waves to soothe her head.

The beach was far less crowded than earlier, and she took off her shoes and tossed them by an empty chair. She walked along the shoreline, not bothering to dodge the tide as it spilled over her feet and up to her ankles.

Her thoughts were running in all directions, all centered on Kelly. The way she felt the instant she saw her on the plane. Their easy conversation on this very beach. Their meals together, laughing and sharing stories of their childhood and friends. The way her body hummed every time Kelly looked at her. The way it came alive when she touched her hand, held her face, kissed her lips. It had been an instant reaction, and that was always dangerous. The flame was incendiary yet could be dangerously explosive at the same time. One minute you could be devoured by the hunger and chewed up and spit out the next. Was that what was happening? She didn't know anything about Kelly, and admittedly they were in paradise, where the real world didn't exist. Had it intruded into their idyllic dream in the form of ugly jealousy?

Matt had no idea, and it hurt her head and her heart to think about it. As she turned around and headed back to her room, she formulated a plan of how she would talk to Kelly about it. They had spent wonderful days exploring the island and intimate nights discovering hidden desires and sinful pleasures. She knew these two weeks were just an engineered diversion from everyday life, one that had a definite conclusion. But, right or wrong, Matt wasn't ready for it to end.

"Matt!" Becca exclaimed, running toward her the minute she stepped in the room. "Where have you been? Is your phone on?"

Matt's heart began to race. She'd never seen Becca this upset. "What's going on?" she asked, reaching for her phone. Both her ringer and vibration were in the *Off* position.

"You need to call Jordan's camp right away."

A sense of déjà vu spread over Matt. Why would the camp be calling her unless something had happened to him?

"What is it? What happened?" Matt asked, frantically searching for the number in her contacts.

"They wouldn't tell me, but when they couldn't get ahold of you, they called me as the backup contact." After an eternity, Matt found the number and hit the dial button.

"This is Mattingly Parker." Her voice was much calmer than she felt. "I got a message you were trying to contact me. Is my son Jordan all right? He's in the nine-and-ten-year-old class. Has something happened to him?" Matt knew she was asking question after question, not giving the man on the other end of the line time to answer any of them.

The world started to spin, and Matt had to sit down on the couch behind her. She listened, then said, "I'll be there as soon as I can."

"Mattie, what is it? You're scaring us." Becca placed her hand on Matt's forearm.

"Jordan's in the hospital. I have to go."

"What?" Sandra asked, sitting down beside her on the couch. "Mattie, what happened?"

"I'm not sure," Matt said as she jumped up and headed toward her room to pack. "It was the camp director. Something about a zipline and crashing into a tree." Matt had only heard bits and pieces of the explanation after the director of the camp told her about the accident.

"Is he okay?"

"He's un…he's unconscious," Matt stuttered. The thought of her son lying on the ground broken and bleeding while she was thousands of miles away caused a gaping hole in her stomach.

"Oh, my God, is he going to be all right?" Becca asked again.

"I have no fucking idea," Matt said sharply. Adrenaline shot through her. "I'm sorry, I didn't mean to snap at you."

"It's okay," Becca said, reaching out and grasping Matt's hand. "The director said he was unconscious when the ambulance came. The hospital will call me when he gets there. Where is my fucking passport?" Matt yanked open the drawers on the dresser.

"You get packed, and I'll call the airline," Becca said.

Matt's heart was pounding as she tossed her suitcase onto the bed, her thoughts centered around her son. The day he was born, his first steps, waving good-bye to Andrea as she walked through the security screening line, standing at the graveside as they lowered his mother into the ground. Matt had explained what was going to happen in terms a three-year-old could understand, but it had been apparent he really didn't understand. He did know that it was something serious, and he had stood quietly beside Matt, holding tightly to her hand. Andrea would have been proud of her little man when he said thank you to the color-guard soldier that had presented him the flag that had been draped over his mother's coffin.

Matt's knees threatened to buckle, and she sat down hard on the bed. "I can't lose him too."

Sandra sat down beside her and squeezed her hand. "He's a tough kid. Whatever it is, he'll pull through."

"If I lose him..."

"You won't." Sandra's voice was stern. "Don't think like that. Do you know where they took him?"

Matt squinted, trying to remember the name of the hospital the director said they were transporting him. "Western Regional, I think. Jesus, he's all alone." Matt sobbed.

"He knows you're with him," Sandra said.

"I got you on the last seat on the seven-fifteen flight," Becca said from the doorway. She looked at her watch. "Get your stuff together. Take only what you need. We'll bring the rest. You connect in Miami, and I have a car waiting for you in Phoenix. It'll drive you directly to the hospital."

Matt's phone rang, and all three of them jumped, startled by the sound. Matt's hand shook as she pressed the Accept icon on the screen. She pushed the speaker icon right after.

Matt's pulse raced as the nurse told her about Jordan's condition. Words like head trauma, concussion, and intracranial bleed made her stomach heave. "Pull it together, Mattingly," she mumbled to herself.

"I'm out of the country," Matt said, after answering what seemed like a thousand questions from the nurse. "I can't get there until…" she looked at Becca.

"Seven a.m."

"Seven a.m. tomorrow morning." Suddenly it occurred to Matt that she'd be on a plane for hours not knowing what was going on with her son.

"I'm sorry," Matt said. "What was your name again?" Matt made the motion of writing something down, and Becca dashed out of the room. She came back an instant later with a pen and a tour brochure. Matt wrote down the nurse's name and phone number.

"I'll be on a plane, so I need to give medical power of attorney to Sandra Howser."

Sandra nodded her understanding.

"I can't sign any form," Matt told the nurse. "But I can send you something in writing as soon as I hang up. She has my authority for any and all medical decisions until I get there. Is that clear?" It was a drastic measure, but she had no alternative.

"He'll be okay," Sandra said after Matt hung up.

Matt turned and looked at Becca, then settled on Sandra. "I said you because you're the tough-as-nails lawyer, but I want both of you to decide whatever he needs." Matt realized she wasn't making much sense, but her friends knew what she meant and what she would want.

"Log into your email when you get on the plane," Sandra said. "We'll keep in touch that way." The ability to send or receive email while Matt was over the Atlantic was almost nonexistent, but it was the only way they could communicate.

"Get dressed," Becca told Matt in her no-nonsense voice. "You have a flight to catch."

❖

"Holy Christ." Becca sighed as she watched from the observation deck as Matt's plane roared down the runway. They were standing close, their shoulders touching. "Please let her get there in time."

"From your lips to God's ears." Sandra put her arm around Becca's shoulders. "I don't want to have to—"

"Hey," Becca said. "We know what Mattie wants, and we'll make any decisions together."

Matt's hands had been shaking so bad she could barely sign the brief, yet effective medical power of attorney Sandra had written on a piece of hotel stationery.

They watched the plane until it disappeared into the horizon.

Chapter Twenty-nine

M a'am, you need to turn off your phone."
Matt bit back her retort. The flight attendant was only doing his job, but this was her lifeline to Jordan, and turning it off was much too close to turning off everything that was keeping her son alive.

The doctor had called as they were approaching the security screening line. Jordan was in a medically induced coma, giving his brain a chance to rest. He was on a ventilator to help him breathe so his body could focus on healing. This news had almost brought Matt to her knees.

She put her phone in airplane mode and didn't even try to stop the tears from streaming down her cheeks as the plane taxied down the runway.

It felt like an eternity before Matt heard the familiar ding indicating it was safe to use electronic devices.

"Come on, come on," she muttered under her breath, impatient for her phone to connect with the plane's network. The huge man to her left glanced her way, obviously perturbed. Too fucking bad. If he and the woman sitting next to the window weren't sixty pounds overweight, maybe he'd be more comfortable squeezed into the middle seat. It was clear who wore the pants in that relationship.

Six new messages lit up, all from Becca and all with the header "No New News." Matt opened them and read the short messages of encouragement from her two best friends. She emailed back her thanks and tried not to squeeze the life out of her phone while she waited for any news.

"Would you please stop fidgeting," the man beside her said indignantly, as if this was his personal aircraft. He had an accent Matt didn't recognize and bad breath.

"Not that it's any of your business, but I just got word that my nine-year-old son is in a coma in Phoenix. This is the last open seat for three days, and if I want to fidget, as you called it, I will. Either get over it or not. I don't really care."

Matt had no idea where her quiet, yet strong outburst came from, but by the look on the man's face, she'd made her point. His wife muttered something about rude just before Matt put on her noise-cancelling headphones, shutting out the world around her.

The flight was smooth but made excruciatingly longer by her constant checking of her phone for a new email from Becca. Nothing but several "No News." Finally one popped up with the heading "Update." Matt felt liked she was going to be sick as she opened it.

Mattie,

Spoke with the doctor. No change, which at this point is a good sign. It means no additional swelling in his brain and his vitals are good. They flew him to Phoenix Children's Hospital. He's in ICU. I know you wouldn't want Cynthia and Harrison there without you, so I called Diane Hecker to go sit with him. I know she was his favorite teacher and a friend of yours, and you wouldn't want him to be alone. She's on her way and will give him your love the minute she gets there.

Matt had become good friends with Diane after Jordan had been in her class in the second grade. Matt's stomach clenched. She glanced at her watch. She'd been in the air almost three hours. She hoped Diane was holding her son's hand right now.

Matt shifted in her seat and a muscle rebelled. She tried to get comfortable, but every time she moved, she was anything but. *Oh my God*, Matt thought, suddenly remembering. *Kelly.* She'd torn out of the resort and off the island without giving her a single thought.

Matt hit Reply, thanking them for thinking about Diane. Matt's mind was on nothing but her son. She ended her note by saying, if they ran into Kelly, to tell her she was sorry for not saying good-bye.

The flight was agonizingly long and the connecting one even longer. If Matt had a dollar for each time she checked her email, she probably could have paid for this trip. She was the first out of her seat when the captain turned off the seat-belt sign. She grabbed her bag from the overhead compartment. Fellow passengers clogged the aisle, and she gritted her teeth to keep from yelling at them to hurry the fuck up and get out.

Finally free of the jetway, she ran through the terminal, not caring who stared at her. She'd packed only her toiletries and her laptop, so she bypassed baggage claim and ran out to the curb. A tall man in a black suit was standing in front of a black sedan, holding a sign with her name on it. When she approached, he quickly opened the rear passenger door and hustled around and climbed into the driver's seat.

"Good morning, Ms. Parker. I'm Eric, and I'll get you to the hospital as quick as I can."

True to his word, they pulled into the front drive ten minutes later.

Matt reached for her bag to get her wallet.

"No need, ma'am. Everything is taken care of."

Eric hurried to her door and offered his hand to help her out of the car.

"Thank you," Matt managed to say.

"My prayers are with you and your family ma'am," he said, causing Matt to stop just before she went inside.

"Thank you, Eric. For everything."

Matt stopped by the front desk just long enough to ask the location of the intensive-care unit. She didn't bother waiting for the elevator but bolted up the stairs two at a time. She pulled open the heavy door with a large white 8 painted in the center.

Her lungs were thick with tension, and she took several deep breaths as she approached the main nurses' desk. A middle-aged woman dressed in light-blue scrubs with cartoon giraffes on them looked up.

"I'm Mattingly Parker. My son is Jordan Parker."

"Yes, Ms. Parker. We've been expecting you. Come with me." She rose from her chair and walked around the large desk cluttered with papers, a stethoscope, and rolls of medical tape. "My name is Kathy, and I've been Jordan's nurse on the night shift."

Matt relaxed at the confident tone in the woman's voice as she gave Matt the rundown on Jordan's condition.

"He's stable, but he's still in a medically induced coma. He's off the ventilator and is getting oxygen to help him breathe," she said quietly.

Matt's stomach tightened. This was not good. It had been over twenty-four hours since the accident, and the longer he was in a coma, the longer his recovery would take.

"He has some bruising around his eyes and the side of his head. His cheek has stitches, but we had an excellent plastic surgeon work on him. He looks a little rough now, but once the swelling goes down, the scars will barely be noticeable. He has a monitor in his head that measures the pressure in his brain." She pointed to her own head. "There is some swelling, though, and the doctor is keeping a close eye on it."

Matt was anxious to be with Jordan, but she knew Kathy was preparing her for what she'd see when she parted the curtain that filled the doorway.

"Thank you. Anything else I should know?" Like when will he wake up, talk, walk again, have a family of his own, grow old?

"Your friend Ms. Hecker has been with him since he was admitted. She wouldn't leave, not even to get a cup of coffee."

Relief and gratitude swept through Matt. She'd been worried sick that Jordan would wake up alone, confused and frightened.

"Thank you, Kathy, and thank you for taking good care of him." Matt braced herself, then pushed aside the curtain.

The lights were low, the morning sun coming through the window. Diane was curled up in a chair that was extended almost flat. Matt murmured a silent thank you.

Her breath caught in her throat when she saw Jordan lying on crisp white sheets, covered with a pale-blue blanket. His head was bandaged in white gauze, an odd-looking tube protruding from the right side of his head. His eyes were swollen almost shut, and the bruising was more than she expected. An oxygen mask on his face partially obscured the white bandage that covered most of his left cheek. He had several cuts on his chin that would heal on their own. The rise and fall of his chest reassured Matt that her son was still breathing, the blip of the heart monitor steady.

He looked so small in the big bed that Matt couldn't help but start to cry. She must have made noise, because Diane sat up quickly, first looking at Jordan, then at her.

"Oh my God, Matt. You're here." She wrapped her in a warm embrace.

Matt wanted to collapse from relief, but the end was far from over.

"Diane, I can't thank you enough for being here. I don't know what I'd have—"

"Hush," Diane said, squeezing her one more time before letting her go. "No thanks are necessary. I'm glad Becca called me. I absolutely adore Jordan, and there was no question I'd come." She took Matt's hand and led her to the chair on the opposite side of the bed. "Come sit down and talk to him. He'll know you're here."

Matt didn't sit but took his hand and leaned over and kissed his uninjured cheek.

"Jordan, Mom's here."

Chapter Thirty

K elly?"

She was sitting on a lounge chair staring across the water. She'd come out to the beach early this morning hoping to see Matt. Why, she didn't know. Matt had never arrived for dinner, and after an hour, and two phone calls, Kelly had returned to her room. She ordered room service, and now the practically untouched tray was sitting in the hall waiting to be picked up.

She'd alternated between hurt, then anger, and back to hurt again all evening. Wasn't she worth at least a phone call? Or, at the very minimum, an impersonal text? She hadn't been stood up since the Valentine's Day dance in tenth grade. She didn't like how it made her feel then and certainly didn't now. "What a selfish coward" was one of the many phrases she'd muttered most of the night while thinking about how inconsiderate Matt was. Their relationship wasn't a forever thing, but she was more than just a booty call. At least she thought she was.

This was the last thing she'd expected from Matt. Kelly had known her to be nothing but kind, thoughtful, and considerate. Or at least she'd thought she was. Did Matt actually believe that just because Kelly had shown a spark of jealousy, she was going to become a stalker? She was anything but, but Matt had no way of knowing that. They were barely acquainted. So why had she tossed and turned all night? Why did it matter? Why did she matter?

She didn't like the way they'd parted yesterday. She was jealous and didn't have a clue how to handle the emotion. Throw in a little fear about how she was starting to feel about Matt, with a bunch of anger at herself because of it, and it was the perfect storm. Unfortunately, Matt had been in the middle of it. It was a stupid, unfair thing to do, but it had snuck up on her so fast, she hadn't seen it coming and could do nothing to stop it. She was dangerously close to falling hard for Matt, which would only get her heartache. They lived on different sides of the country, and even though planes flew both ways, she had a business and could not and would not leave Atlanta. But Matt was an author. Couldn't authors write anywhere? Kelly shook her head. It was equally stupid to think Matt would pack up and move. She had a life in Phoenix, the details of which Kelly knew nothing.

Kelly sensed something major in Matt's life that she hadn't shared with her, and she finally admitted to herself that it bothered her. In the next minute she acknowledged that she had no right to any more than Matt had already given. However, she wanted to know, to do more than peek into her life. She wanted to hear the story behind her favorite old comfy shirt, look through the box of her childhood keepsakes, the charities she supported. Did she complain when she was sick or suffer in silence? Did she pray to God, go to church, sing in the choir? Did she cherish her parents—were her parents even alive? The list was endless, just as the night had been.

"Kelly?"

The question pulled Kelly away from her thoughts. "Hi." Becca was standing at the foot of her chair. She couldn't help herself. She looked past her for Matt.

"Can I talk to you for a minute?"

"Yeah, sure." Her senses told her something was up. She shifted her legs so Becca could sit at her feet. The chairs on either side of her were occupied by towels and sun hats.

"It's about Mattie," Becca said.

"What about her?" Kelly asked without any exterior sign of emotion. Her insides, on the other hand, were churning.

"She had to leave yesterday. There was an accident, and she had to get home."

Kelly sat up straight, alarmed. "Is she all right? Did something happen to her?"

"Her son was hurt in an accident. He's in the hospital."

"Her...son?" *Her son? She never told me she had a son. Why didn't she tell me? Why would she?*

"Yes. He was at a summer camp, and something happened during an activity. We put her on a plane last night."

"Is he okay?" *My God, what Matt must be going through.* She was still trying to get her head around the fact that she even had a son.

"Too soon to know for sure, but all signs are good."

"Is Matt okay?"

"As panicked and worried as you'd expect a mother to be."

"Matt's a mother," Kelly said, still getting used to the idea. That was a big deal. A very big deal.

"She didn't have time to find you and say good-bye, and she asked us to tell you she was sorry about that."

"Sorry? There's no need for her to apologize."

Kelly chastised herself for all the mean things she'd thought about Matt when she hadn't shown up for dinner. God, how selfish.

"Of course her son is her priority. What's his name?"

"Jordan." Becca shrugged. "Andrea wanted to name him after Mattie, but she wouldn't allow it, so they settled on Jordan, after her father."

"How old is he?"

"Nine."

"Nine?" Kelly exclaimed. *Holy shit, Matt has a nine-year-old?* She did the quick math. When Matt's wife died, she was left to raise a three-year-old. Or was she? If Matt hadn't told her about her son, what made her believe her story about a dead wife was real?

"She never told me she had a son." Kelly knew she sounded defensive and had no right to be.

"What was the point?" Becca asked.

"Excuse me?"

"What was the point?" Becca asked again. "She was only going to be here for two weeks and then go home. Weren't you just having a little fun?"

"Excuse me?" Kelly said again, this time more indignant.

"Forgive me if I got this wrong or if I'm out of line, but wasn't this just a vacation fling? No strings, no commitments?"

Even though that's exactly what it was, Becca's words were cold and hard. Kelly had really enjoyed getting to know Matt and had foolishly started to think about the possibility of something more.

"Is that what Matt said it was?"

"Matt didn't tell us much of anything," Becca replied. "But how could it be anything more? She has her son to think about."

Ouch, that hurt. She doubted Becca meant it the way it sounded, but it was true. No way was anyone other than her son number one on her priority list.

"Of course, it was," Kelly lied. She hoped her acting skills were still sharp. "Does she even have a dead wife?" Kelly was aghast she'd asked that question. It'd just shot out of her mouth before she could stop it. Kelly lifted her hand to her mouth. "Oh my God. That was a terrible thing to say. I'm sorry."

Becca looked at her as if preparing for battle. "Yes, she does. Andrea was killed six years ago."

"And she's been raising their son."

"Yes. Sandra and I are around, but she's been pretty much on her own. Her in-laws live across the street, but they're nothing but busybodies trying to tell Mattie how to live her life."

Kelly didn't know what to think, and she certainly didn't know what she was feeling. They'd left on rocky terms, but Kelly was looking forward to making it up to her all night and until they had to leave. The sex was off-the-charts good, but the way Matt looked at her completely took her breath away.

Kelly didn't believe in love at first sight. At least she didn't think she did. When Matt had commented about the book she was reading on the plane, Kelly had looked up into the most vibrant, enticing eyes she'd ever seen. Heat had flashed through her body and lasted long after Matt had taken her seat. Was it basic biology or something more? She felt like a schoolgirl with her first crush. She remembered every word Matt had said and had replayed them all back last night in her room. Just the thought of Matt made her heart race and her stomach flutter. And the sex—my God, the sex was amazing.

Even their first time together had been perfect. Though typically she endured the customary fumbling with clothes and sometimes painful, yet always embarrassing, inadvertent crashing of body parts, her coupling with Matt had been smooth and familiar, like two lovers reunited after months apart. Matt knew just where to touch her, when she needed a firm stroke or a feather-light tease. And, my God, her mouth seemed to be made for Kelly's complete pleasure.

"Are you all right?" Becca placed her hand on Kelly's forearm, as if pulling her back to the here and now.

"Yes, I'm fine," Kelly answered, trying to get her breathing under control. "Please give her my best and tell her I'll be thinking about her." That was absolutely no lie. Kelly would never forget these past ten days.

Several moments passed, and Becca started to get up.

"Wait." Kelly rummaged around in her bag, pulled out a small spiral notebook, and tore out a piece of paper. She brushed off the sand and wrote her name and phone number, then handed it to Becca without hesitation.

"Tell her..." Kelly stopped, unsure what she wanted to tell Matt. That she'd loved their time together? That riding bikes into town was the most fun she'd had in a long time? That watching the sunset was beautiful and making love to the sunrise was breathtaking? Or something as simple as "call me"?

Becca was looking down at her expectantly. "Just tell her I'll be thinking about her, and I hope all goes well with her son."

Becca didn't leave, and Kelly didn't know what else there was to say. Becca sat back down.

"You can tell me to mind my own business or even go to hell, but I've known Mattie for a long time." Becca hesitated, and she had Kelly's complete attention. "I haven't seen her this happy in years."

"What's not to be happy about a vacation fling?" Kelly asked, trying to reassemble her defenses. "No commitment, no strings. Just great sex, if you're lucky." Kelly shifted her gaze back to the horizon, afraid if she blinked, the tears she'd fought to control would spill.

"She hasn't been with anyone since Andrea died."

Kelly turned to look at Becca so fast, she felt dizzy. She hadn't been with anyone for six years? What did that mean? That she couldn't, didn't want to? Was she still so much in love she didn't even think of touching another woman? But she had touched her, made love to her.

"She pretended she had, but we know her too well."

"Why would she do that?" Matt certainly didn't seem to be rusty in the sex department.

"She loved Andrea very much."

Kelly's heart fell at the simple statement. She didn't say anything. She couldn't compete against a dead woman. In a divorce, the love died, but in this case it had been the person. The love lived on.

"I guess she wasn't ready. She had a lot of things going on. She had pressure from the army, her in-laws. And raising a child is not an easy feat."

"The army? Where does the army fit in?"

"Andrea was a nurse. She was stationed in the Middle East and was killed."

"Jesus." Kelly couldn't even imagine how that must hurt.

"She just shut up into herself and went on raising Jordan. This was her first time away from Jordan and the pressure she's under since Andrea died."

The impact of the last few minutes hit Kelly like a blow to the chest. The impact of the past ten days on Matt wasn't lost on her. What must she have been thinking? Feeling? Remembering? Was it her face she saw when Matt closed her eyes or her dead wife's? Were Kelly's hands, fingers, and mouth giving her pleasure, or was it her wife's? She wanted to throw up.

"She didn't tell you any of this?" Becca asked, sounding sympathetic.

"Why would she?" Kelly snapped. "You said it yourself, vacation fling." And what an idiot she'd been to think it might be something else.

"Kelly—"

"Thanks for telling me about Matt." Kelly found her book in her bag and opened it, ending any further conversation.

CHAPTER THIRTY-ONE

K elly put on an acceptable show of excitement as she answered everyone's questions about her trip. Hillary had gathered all her friends together at a local pub, and even though Kelly was exhausted and emotionally drained from the last few days, she graciously accepted. If she hadn't, she'd be answering the same questions a dozen times.

She told funny stories of people on the beach, in the restaurants, and during her wild cab rides. She talked about pedaling bikes into town, riding Waverunners, and skimming over waves on a catamaran. However, she left out one critical detail—that she had done all of this with one woman. One extraordinary woman. She didn't want to think about Matt or feel the resulting gaping hole that had developed in her when her plane lifted off the island. She wanted to put Matt out of her mind, and hopefully that would push her out of her heart as well.

While everyone drank and munched on appetizers, Kelly felt Hillary's eyes on her for most of the evening. Luckily, she waited until they stood by Kelly's car before she began her twenty questions.

"What happened? And don't tell me nothing. I know you better than that, and don't even think of lying to me."

"I met someone."

Three simple words, when spoken, could fill a huge outdoor stadium. Those words signified something meaningful. Something with potential. They meant much more than a simple hookup or short-term thing. The possibilities in those three little words were almost as powerful as the three big ones.

"Did you get her number?" she asked after Kelly had given her the *Cliff Notes* version of her trip.

Kelly shook her head as she zipped her jacket, the breeze cool tonight.

"Where does she live?"

"Nowhere near here."

"So? Planes fly both ways," Hillary said matter-of-factly.

"She has a nine-year-old son."

Hillary frowned. "I didn't see that one coming. Was he there? She didn't take him to a lesbian resort, did she?"

"No. Of course not."

Hillary nodded. "Well, that adds a layer of complicated, but not one that you can't overcome."

"And a wife who was a nurse in the army and was killed in Afghanistan."

"Okay." Hillary drew out the word. "And you two…?"

"She was wonderful, gorgeous, funny, smart, charming."

"And?"

"And, like an idiot, I fell for her." Kelly paused, gathering her courage. Once she said the next word, it was going to be real. "Hard."

The entire flight home, while other passengers had been reminiscing about their vacation or napping, Kelly had been trying not to fall through the chasm that had appeared when Becca sat down at her feet.

"Does that mean there's no chance of anything between you two?"

"She left before I did, and we didn't have a chance to talk about anything or even say good-bye."

"Well, that's pretty shitty." Hillary never shied away from voicing her opinion.

"No. She got a call that her son was in an accident and caught the next flight out."

"Is he okay?"

"I don't know. I hope so."

"How does she feel about you?"

Two cars drove by, obviously looking for a parking space. "Again, I don't know. The last time we were together, we parted on a sour note." Kelly felt the ridiculousness of her jealousy again as she told Hillary that story.

"And you didn't get a chance to talk to her after that?" Hillary asked .

"Her son is enough for her to deal with right now. I'm not going to add to her problems. And besides, we agreed it was just vacation sex. Just fun, no commitment."

"And how was the sex?" Hillary asked, bumping her shoulder.

Warmth spread through Kelly at the kaleidoscope of memories that flashed in her head. They took her breath away. "Earth-shattering does not even begin to describe it," Kelly said, her voice choked with emotion.

"Then use other words," Hillary teased. "Lots of other words."

Kelly remained quiet. Normally she discussed everything with Hillary, but this was different. She wanted to keep it all to herself. It wasn't the pain or embarrassment of falling when she knew there was no guardrail, but what she had shared and felt with Matt was so extraordinary, so one of a kind, she didn't want to share it with anyone. At least not yet.

"She was that special?" Hillary asked seriously.

Kelly nodded and stopped trying to stifle the tears that had threatened to spill out all day.

CHAPTER THIRTY-TWO

The flash from the cameras was blinding. Why had she agreed to this? It had turned into a three-ring circus, with the lesbian activists in one, the US Army in the other, and she and Jordan in the middle.

The call had come several months ago, the one she'd thought was a hoax until she realized it wasn't. A review of events around Andrea's death had resulted in her being posthumously awarded the nation's highest recognition of bravery, the Medal of Honor. What had taken six years? Was it because she was a woman? A nurse? A lesbian?

Matt was angry, but she'd stowed her reaction away for the sake of Jordan. He looked so proud as he stood at attention, with his fresh haircut, solemn expression, and his mother's camo uniform on his thin, gangly body as the President of the United States placed his mother's medal around his neck. Standing beside him, Matt didn't hear the words the president said to him, only the kind understanding in her eyes. Four others were also receiving the honor, but they had come home. Andrea had not.

Matt glanced around the room. Sitting in the front row were her mom and dad, Andrea's parents, and immediate family members of the other award recipients. The remaining rows were reserved for friends and various dignitaries. She panned the crowd for Becca and Sandra. They'd talked before the ceremony began, and she'd expected them to be seated directly behind her parents. Matt frowned when she saw them all the way in the last row. Why were they back there? Before she could think of anything else, the man in front of them shifted, and a familiar face came into view.

The world around her dimmed, and voices faded in the background as her singular focus was on Kelly, sitting beside Becca. Her smile was shy, as if she wasn't sure she belonged here. Becca leaned over and whispered something in her ear, and Kelly nodded.

Matt's heart pounded. What was she doing here? What did it mean? How did she know? Those, and a thousand other questions, flashed through her brain like lightning during a summer storm. She'd never thought she'd see Kelly again, and her heart soared. Applause jarred her focus back to the event, and she and Jordan took their seats to listen to the obligatory speeches.

Matt tried to pay attention to the dignitaries, politicians, and high-ranking military as they spoke, their speeches peppered with words like honor, bravery, and sacrifice. Uncharacteristically, Jordan sat perfectly still, his eyes riveted on the heavy gold star surrounded by a green wreath hanging from the ribbon around his neck. The star had five points, each suspended from a gold bar with the inscription VALOR. His mother's name was inscribed on the back.

Matt's heart clenched at the injustice of her son not having his hero mother in his life. She didn't care about the additional pension he received as her dependent, the commissary and exchange privileges, or even the admission he was entitled to at one of the US service academies. What was important to her was that Jordan would never forget his mother and her sacrifice to others. She knew without a doubt that he would follow in his mother's footsteps.

The ceremony came to a close, and after more photos and handshakes, they retreated to another room down the hall. Jordan was showing the medal to Harrison, while Cynthia stood stiffly beside him.

"Andrea would have been so humbled," Becca said as she hugged Matt.

Sandra was next. "She was so proud of being a soldier."

"Thanks," Matt said, unable to take her eyes off Kelly, who was standing slightly behind Becca. She still looked uncomfortable and unsure if she were welcome.

"Let's go talk to Jordan." Becca pulled Sandra's arm, leaving them alone.

Matt's mouth was suddenly dry as she approached Kelly.

"It was a beautiful ceremony," Kelly said almost reverently.

Warmth flooded Matt at the sound of the voice she thought she'd hear again only in her dreams.

"Yes, it was," she somehow managed to say. "How…"

"Becca tracked me down," Kelly said, explaining how she was standing in front of her. "She insisted that I come."

"She can be persuasive," Matt said, forever grateful Becca was.

Kelly looked back and forth from Jordan to the large photo of Andrea on the easel in the front of the room. "She's beautiful," Kelly said. "He looks just like her."

"Yes, he does." Matt's heart warmed. She saw the resemblance more and more every day. "He's exactly like her too."

"Quite a young man."

"He is definitely his own man. I know he gets teased a lot in school, but he doesn't care."

"You should be very proud. Is he okay?" Kelly returned her gaze to Matt. "Becca said he was hurt?"

"He's fine now. It was touch-and-go for a few days, but kids bounce back pretty quickly." Matt recalled how panicked she'd felt until she saw him with her own eyes. "Some scrapes and bruises, but he was up and about in a few days and wanting to finish the summer at camp." They'd argued when she'd said no. "He wants to go to West Point."

"Does that scare you?" Kelly asked intuitively.

"To death. But I have a few years to get used to it."

They stood there, and Matt wanted to know why she was here, why she had agreed to come, but she didn't want to break the sheer comfort of just having Kelly near her.

Well-wishers and those offering their sympathy for her loss interrupted them several times. A thin man in a military dress uniform slowly approached her, uncertainty written all over his face. He stopped, snapped to attention, and saluted her. Matt didn't know what she should do.

"Ms. Parker," he said after relaxing. "My name is Sergeant Maxwell Young. I had the pleasure of serving with your wife at Aid Station, Greenway. She was an outstanding officer, ma'am."

"Thank you, Sergeant." Greenway was the base where Andrea was killed. Kelly started to step away, but Matt grabbed her hand, silently imploring her to stay.

"Ma'am, Captain Underwood saved my life, and I, and my family, are forever grateful."

"Andrea loved being a nurse and helping people." Matt repeated the words others had said to her so many times. "I'm glad she could help you when you needed it."

The soldier grew hesitant, then straightened, pain on his face.

"No, ma'am. You misunderstood. Captain Underwood saved my life. I was the one she was going after when she was…" Sergeant Young was struggling with his words. "When she was hit. Please accept my deepest sympathies to you and your son."

In the days after Andrea was killed, Matt often wondered what she would say or do if she ever met the person she had died trying to save. In one scenario she would scream and rant and blame him for ruining her life, blame him for Jordan growing up without knowing how wonderful his mother was. But now that the man was in front of her, she did neither. She simply extended her hand. "Thank you, Sergeant. Your coming here today to honor Andrea means a lot to me and our son. You are very brave."

Matt saw him visibly relax, as if anticipating she would scream at him or strike him in anger. No way could she do that. Not now.

"It's not your fault, Sergeant." Matt's voice was strong, her conviction firm. "I never thought it was. Like Andrea, you were simply in the wrong place at the wrong time. I hope you are doing well?"

Matt knew a little about post-traumatic stress disorder and the toll it took on service members and their families. She in no way wanted to assume this man suffered from it, but how could he not?

"Yes, ma'am. A little better every day. Even more so today," he said solemnly, glancing at Andrea's picture, then back at her. "I don't want to take up any more of your time, ma'am. My sympathies again."

"Thank you, Sergeant. Please take care."

Matt watched as the man walked away, stopped in front of Andrea's picture, saluted, then walked out of the room.

"That was powerful."

Matt was so overcome with emotion at the soldier's story, she'd forgotten Kelly was beside her. "Yes, it was. He's a brave man. I hope he's doing okay."

Kelly squeezed her hand. "I think he will be now."

Matt looked down at their hands, fingers entwined. She brought Kelly's hand up and kissed her knuckles. "Thank you for coming."

Kelly didn't respond for several beats. When she did, she asked, "Why didn't you tell me?"

Pain stabbed Matt in the heart. "Which? That I had a nine-year-old son, or my wife was killed saving somebody else?"

"Both, I suppose, but I understand now why you didn't."

"It definitely would have been a real mood killer," Matt joked.

"No. That's not it."

Matt looked at Kelly, puzzled.

"It's very personal, and we weren't in a place where we were sharing personal."

Matt chuckled and kissed Kelly's hand again. "If I'm not mistaken, we were as personal as two people can get. Many, many, many times, as a matter of fact." She flushed all over at the memory.

"How dare you sully my daughter's name." Matt turned. Cynthia was standing right behind her, her face contorted in rage.

Cynthia looked at Kelly's hand in hers, then back at her, with something in her eyes Matt had never seen. It took an instant for Matt to realize what she'd known all along, and it didn't scare her. Kelly was worth fighting for.

"Cynthia," Harrison interjected. Matt didn't know where he came from. "Stop it."

"I will not stop it," she spat, her teeth clenched. "We are here honoring my daughter, and she had the nerve to bring her…"

"Be careful what you say, Cynthia," Matt warned her.

"I know exactly what I'm saying." She growled.

Matt interrupted her. "Then say it somewhere else. This is not the time and definitely not the place. If you truly want to honor your daughter, then you'll keep your opinions to yourself until we get outside and away from my son."

She'd had enough of Cynthia's sanctimonious attitude regarding her daughter and how Matt should carry on her life without her. She had no idea who her daughter was. She'd never spent a minute alone with her the entire time Matt and Andrea were together. She'd never told her she was proud of her or of her allegiance to her country. Not once had she told Andrea that she was honored that her daughter was serving her country, one that took her away from her family, her child. A commitment that ultimately got her killed.

Mercifully the event broke up before Cynthia could cause a scene, and Matt found herself outside face-to-face with her. Becca was her wingman, Sandra next to Kelly. Jordan was already in the car, talking animatedly on FaceTime with his friends.

"And just how am I dishonoring Andrea's memory, Cynthia? Because I'm moving on with my life? Because I'm not wearing black and wallowing in grief over her death? That I didn't curl up and simply exist? Andrea would not want me to do that, and if it were any of your business, which it's not, she specifically made me promise, on more than one occasion, that I would not stop living. That I would find someone to love and who would love Jordan as much as she did." She was so angry her hands were shaking.

"My daughter is dead because of you," Cynthia spat.

"Me? She did nothing because of me," Matt said. This confrontation was getting ugly, and she was powerless to stop it. Nor did she want to.

"Because of you, she thought she had something to prove."

Cynthia wasn't making sense. "How so, Cynthia? She was an honorable soldier and a great mother. She didn't need to prove anything to anyone, including you."

Cynthia blanched. "Because you made her what she was. You turned her against everything that was right and natural."

Cynthia's words were mean and so far from the truth. But Cynthia would never see that, would never understand her daughter was a vibrant woman who had loved other women for years before she met Matt.

"Cynthia, I said that's enough," Harrison said, taking her arm. "Matt, I'm sorry," he said.

"*You* don't have anything to apologize for, Harrison."

"I'm not apologizing for Cynthia. She can either do that or not. I don't care anymore. I'm sorry you've had to deal with this for so long and that I haven't stepped forward and said anything until now."

Harrison's words stunned Matt. He never agreed with his wife, but he never did anything to shut her down or try to change her beliefs either. Why now?

The whipsaw of the last half hour was making Matt's head spin. She needed time to think.

"Dad?" Matt called to her father a few yards away, listening intently but not butting in. He knew Matt could take care of herself. "Dad, would you and Mom take Jordan to the museum? I don't think I'm up to it right now." She'd promised Jordan they'd take him to the Air and Space Museum after the ceremony.

"Sure, honey," he said, looking between her and Kelly. Her parents knew something was up. She'd told them about Kelly shortly after she returned home, and they were supportive in whatever she wanted to do.

"You go back to the hotel and relax. Don't worry about Jordan," her father said.

A few minutes later everyone left, Cynthia stomping back to her car and leaving Matt alone with Kelly.

CHAPTER THIRTY-THREE

"Can we walk?" Matt asked, indicating the wide sidewalk. The crowds were thick, but they seemed to part as they approached. "What are you doing here?" Matt asked as they passed in front of the White House.

Kelly had been asking herself that question ever since she had arrived yesterday. It had been a week since Becca had called her and more than six since she'd seen Matt. Every day had felt like an eternity, each lasting longer than the day before.

She hadn't seen or heard from Becca or Sandra after the morning Becca had told her Matt had left. She almost hadn't answered the unfamiliar number on her phone six weeks later when it rang.

"Kelly, it's Becca."

It took a moment for her brain to connect the name to a face. "Becca, hi. How are you?" She had really liked both Becca and Sandra and could see them being her good friends in a different circumstance. Why was Becca calling?

"I hope I'm not disturbing you. Do you have a minute?"

Kelly glanced at her watch. She was leaning against the counter eating a bowl of cereal and watching Good Morning America. *She had twelve minutes until she needed to leave her house and get to the job site. But she was the boss and could be late if she wanted to. "Sure. I have a few. How have you been?"*

"I'm well, thank you. Keeping busy putting criminals in jail."

"And the citizens of the US appreciate it," Kelly said. *"What's up?"* she asked carefully, not sure she wanted to know the answer. Becca surely wasn't calling just to say hi.

"Sandra and I debated if we should call."

Kelly's heart started to beat faster. Was it Matt? Had something happened to her? Was her son okay? She wasn't going down that road again. She'd just started to pull herself back together after she'd made a complete ass of herself over Matt. She'd never said any of the words, but she'd fallen completely in, way-over-her-head crazy for Matt.

"Obviously you decided to, so tell me." Kelly hoped she sounded disinterested, even though she was anything but. Matt was always on her mind.

"It's about Mattie."

Kelly placed her bowl on the counter and willed her heart to slow down and beat normally.

"Look, Kelly," Becca said, sounding unsure. *"Um, have you talked to her?"*

"No." But I've dreamed about her every night. Longed to hear her voice, see her smile, feel her touch, breathe her air. Jesus, Kelly, STOP!

"She needs you, Kelly."

"Is she okay?" Kelly turned off the TV and sat on one of the bar stools, her legs suddenly weak.

"She is, well, sort of. I mean, nothing's wrong with her, but she's not happy."

Kelly hoped it was because of her, but that would be too good to be true. Just because she'd been miserable ever since Matt left the island didn't mean she was unhappy too.

"She misses you." Becca's words were simple.

"Misses me? She misses me?" Kelly asked, incredulous.

"Yeah."

"Then why hasn't she called?"

"She's afraid to."

"Of what? Me?"

"Well, yes," Becca said hesitantly.

"What in the hell for? I understand why she left. I'm not mad at her." Kelly felt like she was in the fifth grade talking through an intermediary.

"She's afraid you believe your hooking up was just a vacation fling, nothing more. That you won't want anything to do with her. And because of Jordan."

"That she didn't tell me about him or that she has a son?" Kelly didn't address the first part of Becca's statement.

"Both, I think."

"Does she know you're calling me?"

Becca laughed. *"She'd kill me and Sandra if she did."*

"Then why are you?"

"Because we love Mattie, and we haven't seen her as happy as she was when she was with you in a long time. We want to see her that way again."

"What makes you think she didn't view our time together as a vacation fling?" Kelly asked, trying to stay calm. The last thing she needed was to make a fool of herself, again, over a woman who didn't feel the same. It was bad enough to have done it privately, but to put herself out there in front of Matt and be turned away would be devastating.

"Because she can't stop thinking about you. She gets this wistful look in her eyes when she thinks we're not looking. She doesn't laugh, and her smiles are all for show. Even Jordan knows she's different. And he's just a kid."

"What has she said?"

"That's just it. She won't talk about it. She just keeps saying that nothing's wrong, that she's still getting over Jordan's accident and back to her life. But Jordan recovered very quickly, like kids do."

"And you expect me to what, show up on her front doorstep and declare my undying love? Sounds a lot like jumping off a cliff to me." As crazy as it sounded, that's exactly what she wanted to do.

"Well, actually," Becca said, and Kelly listened.

"Becca called me," Kelly said, answering Matt's question as they stepped around a family taking a selfie with the White House in the background.

Matt stopped walking. "She had no right to," Matt said, sounding angry. "She never should have overstepped like that."

Kelly's heart sank into her stomach at Matt's words. She didn't want her here, or anywhere in her life for that matter. After she'd hung up from talking to Becca, Kelly had calculated all the reasons to stay away. Matt lived across the country; she had a child, memories of a wife who had died a hero, and now obligations the military were putting on her. Could she compete with that? Did she want to? These were huge complications she didn't need in her life. Did she want them even if Matt was the prize at the beginning, middle, and end?

But here she was, standing in front of her, and there was no other place she wanted to be. Before she could change her mind, she'd booked a flight and filled out all the necessary paperwork to be allowed into the ceremony. She had a suitcase full of clothes in a hotel room a few miles away.

She pulled herself together. "They're worried about you."

"They?" Matt asked, apparently surprised. "Sandra's in on this too?"

"Would you have expected otherwise?"

"I'll kill them," Matt said, clenching her teeth.

"I don't think you should say something like that when we're this close to the White House," Kelly said, trying to lessen some of the tension between them. They continued to walk, the sidewalk crowded.

"When did she call you?"

"A few weeks ago."

"What did she say?"

"Does it matter?"

"Not if it's pity that brought you here," Matt said shortly.

It was a legitimate question, but Matt's words hurt anyway.

They crossed the street, and Kelly stopped in the shade under a large tree. She turned to face Matt. "Do you want me here?"

"Here is over." Matt lifted her hands toward the White House, indicating the event they'd just come from.

"You know what I mean," Kelly snapped. Her nerves were raw. She was taking all the risk here, and she was teetering on the edge. "Don't be obtuse. Why aren't you answering my question?"

"Do you honestly want to be in the middle of all this?" Matt shot back. "I have a child who idolizes his dead mother, intrusive in-laws, a demanding publisher, meddling friends, and a dog that eats anything that isn't one of her toys."

"I didn't put my business on hold, fly a thousand miles in shitty weather, have the FBI dig into my past and interview everyone I've ever slept with, including Suzanne, and have your mother-in-law insult me because I didn't have anything else to do." She took a deep breath to calm down. It didn't work. She was teetering on a razor-sharp edge that would determine the rest of her life, and she needed a cool head. Well, Kelly thought. I was never good at doing what I needed to do. She jumped.

"I know we said it was only vacation sex, no pressure, no obligations, but I want more. I don't care that you have a child, only that you didn't tell me about him. I get it," Kelly said, raising her hand to stop Matt from interrupting her. "I get that we weren't in a place where that mattered, but it matters now. I understand why he idolizes his mother. He has every right to. I don't care that your in-laws are intrusive. They lost their daughter and don't want to lose her son. I'm a demanding boss, so I know what it's like to have one. Your friends love you, and as long as your dog is house-trained, I don't care." She put her hands on her hips. "Did I miss anything?"

Kelly had to catch her breath. She was good at sidestepping falling objects on a job site, but falling in love with Matt was not one she could have avoided.

"Good," Kelly said when Matt didn't add anything to her list. "Now, to make the playing field even, I've worked my ass off to have a very successful business that I'm not interested in leaving. That's not to say I couldn't open a satellite office in Phoenix. I understand the market is booming. However, I love what I do and am a workaholic if I'm not careful. I don't have many friends because most of them were Suzanne's. I sleep on the left side of the bed, need at least two cups of coffee to function in the morning, so I'm not a fan of morning sex, at least until I met you, and I take really long, really hot showers. I like porn, country music, and stupid disaster movies, and my dog eats out of the cat box if I forget to put the lid back on."

Kelly took another deep breath before the final plunge. "My parents would be heartbroken if I were to move, but they love me and will get over it as long as I go back twice a year to visit. They've always wanted a grandson, and they'll love yours as if he were mine. I don't know how to be a stepmom, but I'm willing to do anything and everything necessary to make sure Jordan knows I love him," Kelly stepped closer and took Matt's face in her hands. She didn't care that they were standing in front of the White House and that anyone could see them. She didn't care that she might go home alone and heartbroken or that she might never love again. Matt was worth everything that stood in her way.

"That he knows I love him," she repeated. She bent her head, and just before their lips met, she whispered, "as much as I love his mother." Then she kissed her.

Matt tried to corral her racing thoughts, but the excitement of Kelly's lips on hers was too overpowering. It had been too long since she'd felt the softness of her body melt into hers, inhale her scent that tormented her during the long nights she lay alone in her bed.

Had she heard her correctly? Somewhere between Kelly saying she wanted more than casual, no-strings vacation sex and that she loved her, Matt had lost her mind.

Kelly's kisses were soft and promising, teasing and demanding. They touched her soul and filled her with confidence and conviction that she was the one she wanted to spend the rest of her life with.

"I don't know how we'll…"

Kelly kissed her again, this time long and hard, erasing everything Matt was planning to say. When she finally lifted her head, they were both breathing heavily.

"I don't either," Kelly said, her eyes filled with love. "But if we want it bad enough, we'll make it work. I want to do homework, sit on hard bleachers with the other parents, and bring soccer-game snacks. I want to build sandcastles in the sand with you and climb mountains and sail into the sunset with you and Jordan by my side. And I want you. Every day in my life and every night in our bed."

"Is that a proposal?" Matt managed to ask, her heart racing so fast she was dizzy.

"Yes."

"Yes."

"Yes what?"

"Yes, I want you here. In my life," Matt said.

Kelly had given her so much without her even knowing it. She'd given Matt her last first date, last first fight, and most important, her last first kiss, and Matt was never so happy to never be doing any of those ever again.

CHAPTER THIRTY-FOUR

Eight years later

"Are you bawling like a baby?" Becca's voice was crystal clear as it came through their car speakers.

"No. I'm crying like any mother who just left her child at West Point." She and Kelly had just dropped Jordan off on the meticulously manicured grounds of the nation's premier military academy. He would spend the next forty-seven months of his life behind these walls learning how to be a soldier. Not just any soldier, an army officer, just like his mother. Matt knew this was the last she'd see of the young man who had dreamed of this day as far back as she could remember.

As he'd grown older, Jordan had developed more and more of Andrea's mannerisms, and his smile was mirrored in every picture of his mother. Time had softened what once was debilitating pain. He still had everything in his room in its exact place, insisted on getting his hair cut every five weeks whether or not it needed it, ironed his clothes with military creases, and had been number one in his ROTC class in high school. He'd never cared what his peers thought of him. Watching him march around the parade grounds in his sparkling new plebe uniform, spit-shined shoes, hat pulled low shading his eyes, she knew he would be his own man as well.

She'd managed to hold back the tears she knew would embarrass Jordan until they got in the car. He'd insisted on no public displays of affection, so she had hugged him and smothered him with kisses before they left the hotel this morning. She'd prepared herself as best any mother could, but the reality was far more painful than she'd imagined.

"Come over and we'll get drunk," Becca said.

Matt turned her head to check Kelly's reaction. Even after eight years, just looking at Kelly made her heart skip and her body warm all over. She was her rock, her inspiration, her tower of strength, and today was no different. Kelly smiled and nodded.

"We'd love to, and considering you're picking us up at the airport makes it even more perfect."

"Then we'll definitely get drunk."

"No, *we* won't. We need to get home to Sara and relieve my parents from babysitting duty. She's probably exhausted them." Matt's parents often babysat their eight-year-old daughter she and Kelly had adopted out of the foster-care system when she was three. Her parents had gladly volunteered while Matt and Kelly accompanied Jordan to New York.

Matt thought about another time when she'd left her son to experience his dream. A lot had happened over that summer. Kelly had come into her life, Becca got engaged, and Sandra fell hard for a woman who wasn't a size eight, didn't get her hair and nails done at a salon, and drove a fifteen-year-old car. Ashley was short, on the frumpy side, and Sandra was completely devoted to her. The feeling was mutual, and next weekend they would be celebrating their seventh wedding anniversary.

"Your parents are fine," Becca said. "Kevin and I stopped by your house last night. Sara was in the tub, and your father was taking a pan of brownies out of the oven." Kevin had in fact asked Becca to marry him shortly after they all returned from their vacation.

"My dad was making brownies?" Matt asked incredulously.

"I don't think he was making them. I think he was simply taking them out of the oven. Anyway, they're fine, and one drink will do you both good."

"And we want to hear all about the big, bad military establishment that's going to brainwash my godchild," Sandra shouted in the background.

Matt had to laugh because, as much as Sandra hated all things governmental, she had pulled in all her contacts to write letters of recommendations for Jordan. As the son of a Medal of Honor recipient, he was entitled to a spot at any of the military academies but was still required to provide five letters attesting to his demonstration of the seven army values: loyalty, duty, respect, selfless service, honor, integrity, and personal courage.

Later that night, after her parents had gone home and Sara was tucked away in her bed, Matt and Kelly finally had a minute to themselves.

"It's going to be kind of quiet around here," Kelly said, her fingers lightly tracing the outline of the tattoo of a bicycle with waves crashing in the distance. Matt had gotten the tattoo eight years ago, after returning from her trip to the Turks and Caicos. Kelly had discovered it the first night they were together in DC, and her heart had burst with love.

Jordan had been an active high-schooler with a lot of friends who were always coming and going. Like her big brother, whom she idolized, when Sara had started school, the neighborhood kids also congregated at the Parker-Newsome house. Matt and Kelly preferred it that way. They could keep a close eye on Sara and her friends. They'd seen too many instances where unattended children and an unmonitored internet resulted in an explosive combination. Jordan's laughter, once filling the house, would exist only in their memories. He would come back to the big house Kelly had built for them, and it would always be his home.

"Actually, I think it's going to be another wonderful summer."

THE END

About the Author

Julie Cannon divides her time by being a corporate suit, wife, mom, sister, friend, and writer. Julie and her wife have lived in at least half a dozen states, traveled around the world, and have an unending supply of dedicated friends. And of course, the most important people in their lives are their three kids: #1, Dude, and the Diving Miss Em.

With the release of *The Last First Kiss*, Julie will have twenty books published by Bold Strokes Books. Her first novel, *Come and Get Me*, was a finalist for the Golden Crown Literary Society Best Lesbian Romance and Début Author awards. Several of her books have additionally been finalists for the GCLS Best Lesbian Romance, and *I Remember* won the GCLS Best Lesbian Romance in 2014. *Rescue Me* and *Wishing on a Dream* were finalists for Best Lesbian Romance from the prestigious Lambda Literary Society.

www.JulieCannon.com

Books Available from Bold Strokes Books

His Brother's Viscount by Stephanie Lake. Hector Somerville wants to rekindle his illicit love affair with Viscount Wentworth, but he must overcome one problem: Wentworth still loves Hector's brother. (978-1-63555-805-0)

Journey to Cash by Ashley Bartlett. Cash Braddock thought everything was great, but it looks like her history is about to become her right now. Which is a real bummer. (978-1-63555-464-9)

Liberty Bay by Karis Walsh. Wren Lindley's life is mired in tradition and untouched by trends until social media star Gina Strickland introduces an irresistible electricity into her off-the-grid world. (978-1-63555-816-6)

Scent by Kris Bryant. Nico Marshall has been burned by women in the past wanting her for her money. This time, she's determined to win Sophia Sweet over with her charm. (978-1-63555-780-0)

Shadows of Steel by Suzie Clarke. As their worlds collide and their choices come back to haunt them, Rachel and Claire must figure out how to stay together and most of all, stay alive. (978-1-63555-810-4)

The Clinch by Nicole Disney. Eden Bauer overcame a difficult past to become a world champion mixed martial artist, but now rising star and dreamy bad girl Brooklyn Shaw is a threat both to Eden's title and her heart. (978-1-63555-820-3)

The Last First Kiss by Julie Cannon. Kelly Newsome is so ready for a tropical island vacation, but she never expects to meet the woman who could give her her last first kiss. (978-1-63555-768-8)

The Mandolin Lunch by Missouri Vaun. Despite their immediate attraction, everything about Garet Allen says short-term, and Tess Hill refuses to consider anything less than forever. (978-1-63555-566-0)

Thor: Daughter of Asgard by Genevieve McCluer. When Hannah Olsen finds out she's the reincarnation of Thor, she's thrown into a world of magic and intrigue, unexpected attraction, and a mystery she's got to unravel. (978-1-63555-814-2)

Veterinary Technician by Nancy Wheelton. When a stable of horses is threatened Val and Ronnie must work together against the odds to save them, and maybe even themselves along the way. (978-1-63555-839-5)

16 Steps to Forever by Georgia Beers. Can Brooke Sullivan and Macy Carr find themselves by finding each other? (978-1-63555-762-6)

All I Want for Christmas by Georgia Beers, Maggie Cummings, Fiona Riley. The Christmas season sparks passion and love in these stories by award winning authors Georgia Beers, Maggie Cummings, and Fiona Riley. (978-1-63555-764-0)

From the Woods by Charlotte Greene. When Fiona goes backpacking in a protected wilderness, the last thing she expects is to be fighting for her life. (978-1-63555-793-0)

Heart of the Storm by Nicole Stiling. For Juliet Mitchell and Sienna Bennett a forbidden attraction definitely isn't worth upending the life they've worked so hard for. Is it? (978-1-63555-789-3)

If You Dare by Sandy Lowe. For Lauren West and Emma Prescott, following their passions is easy. Following their hearts, though? That's almost impossible. (978-1-63555-654-4)

Love Changes Everything by Jaime Maddox. For Samantha Brooks and Kirby Fielding, no matter how careful their plans, love will change everything. (978-1-63555-835-7)

Not This Time by MA Binfield. Flung back into each other's lives, can former bandmates Sophia and Madison have a second chance at romance? (978-1-63555-798-5)

The Dubious Gift of Dragon Blood by J. Marshall Freeman. One day Crispin is a lonely high school student—the next he is fighting a war in a land ruled by dragons, his otherworldly boyfriend at his side. (978-1-63555-725-1)

The Found Jar by Jaycie Morrison. Fear keeps Emily Harris trapped in her emotionally vacant life; can she find the courage to let Beck Reynolds guide her toward love? (978-1-63555-825-8)

Aurora by Emma L McGeown. After a traumatic accident, Elena Ricci is stricken with amnesia leaving her with no recollection of the last eight years, including her wife and son. (978-1-63555-824-1)

Avenging Avery by Sheri Lewis Wohl. Revenge against a vengeful vampire unites Isa Meyer and Jeni Denton, but it's love that heals them. (978-1-63555-622-3)

Bulletproof by Maggie Cummings. For Dylan Prescott and Briana Logan, the complicated NYC criminal justice system doesn't leave room for love, but where the heart is concerned, no one is bulletproof. (978-1-63555-771-8)

Her Lady to Love by Jane Walsh. A shy wallflower joins forces with the most popular woman in Regency London on a quest to catch a husband, only to discover a wild passion for each other that far eclipses their interest for the Marriage Mart. (978-1-63555-809-8)

No Regrets by Joy Argento. For Jodi and Beth, the possibility of losing their future will force them to decide what is really important. (978-1-63555-751-0)

The Holiday Treatment by Elle Spencer. Who doesn't want a gay Christmas movie? Holly Hudson asks herself that question and discovers that happy endings aren't only for the movies. (978-1-63555-660-5)

Too Good to be True by Leigh Hays. Can the promise of love survive the realities of life for Madison and Jen, or is it too good to be true? (978-1-63555-715-2)

Treacherous Seas by Radclyffe. When the choice comes down to the lives of her officers against the promise she made to her wife, Reese Conlon puts everything she cares about on the line. (978-1-63555-778-7)

Two to Tangle by Melissa Brayden. Ryan Jacks has been a player all her life, but the new chef at Tangle Valley Vineyard changes everything. If only she wasn't off the menu. (978-1-63555-747-3)

When Sparks Fly by Annie McDonald. Will the devastating incident that first brought Dr. Daniella Waveny and hockey coach Luca McCaffrey together on frozen ice now force them apart, or will their secrets and fears thaw enough for them to create sparks? (978-1-63555-782-4)

Best Practice by Carsen Taite. When attorney Grace Maldonado agrees to mentor her best friend's little sister, she's prepared to confront Perry's rebellious nature, but she isn't prepared to fall in love. Legal Affairs: one law firm, three best friends, three chances to fall in love. (978-1-63555-361-1)

Home by Kris Bryant. Natalie and Sarah discover that anything is possible when love takes the long way home. (978-1-63555-853-1)

Keeper by Sydney Quinne. With a new charge under her reluctant wing—feisty, highly intelligent math wizard Isabelle Templeton—Keeper Andy Bouchard has to prevent a murder or die trying. (978-1-63555-852-4)

One More Chance by Ali Vali. Harry Basantes planned a future with Desi Thompson until the day Desi disappeared without a word, only to walk back into her life sixteen years later. (978-1-63555-536-3)

Renegade's War by Gun Brooke. Freedom fighter Aurelia DeCallum regrets saving the woman called Blue. She fears it will jeopardize her mission, and secretly, Blue might end up breaking Aurelia's heart. (978-1-63555-484-7)

The Other Women by Erin Zak. What happens in Vegas should stay in Vegas, but what do you do when the love you find in Vegas changes your life forever? (978-1-63555-741-1)

The Sea Within by Missouri Vaun. Time is running out for Dr. Elle Graham to convince Captain Jackson Drake that the only thing that can save future Earth resides in the past, and rescue her broken heart in the process. (978-1-63555-568-4)

To Sleep With Reindeer by Justine Saracen. In Norway under Nazi occupation, Maarit, an Indigenous woman; and Kirsten, a Norwegian resister, join forces to stop the development of an atomic weapon. (978-1-63555-735-0)

Twice Shy by Aurora Rey. Having an ex with benefits isn't all it's cracked up to be. Will Amanda Russo learn that lesson in time to take a chance on love with Quinn Sullivan? (978-1-63555-737-4)

Z-Town by Eden Darry. Forced to work together to stay alive, Meg and Lane must find the centuries-old treasure before the zombies find them first. (978-1-63555-743-5)

Bet Against Me by Fiona Riley. In the high stakes luxury real estate market, everything has a price, and as rival Realtors Trina Lee and Kendall Yates find out, that means their hearts and souls, too. (978-1-63555-729-9)

Broken Reign by Sam Ledel. Together on an epic journey in search of a mysterious cure, a princess and a village outcast must overcome life-threatening challenges and their own prejudice if they want to survive. (978-1-63555-739-8)

Just One Taste by CJ Birch. For Lauren, it only took one taste to start trusting in love again. (978-1-63555-772-5)

Lady of Stone by Barbara Ann Wright. Sparks fly as a magical emergency forces a noble embarrassed by her ability to submit to a low-born teacher who resents everything about her. (978-1-63555-607-0)

Last Resort by Angie Williams. Katie and Rhys are about to find out what happens when you meet the girl of your dreams but you aren't looking for a happily ever after. (978-1-63555-774-9)

Longing for You by Jenny Frame. When Debrek housekeeper Katie Brekman is attacked amid a burgeoning vampire-witch war, Alexis Villiers must go against everything her clan believes in to save her. (978-1-63555-658-2)

Money Creek by Anne Laughlin. Clare Lehane is a troubled lawyer from Chicago who tries to make her way in a rural town full of secrets and deceptions. (978-1-63555-795-4)

Passion's Sweet Surrender by Ronica Black. Cam and Blake are unable to deny their passion for each other, but surrendering to love is a whole different matter. (978-1-63555-703-9)

The Holiday Detour by Jane Kolven. It will take everything going wrong to make Dana and Charlie see how right they are for each other. (978-1-63555-720-6)

Too Hot to Ride by Andrews & Austin. World famous cutting horse champion and industry legend Jane Barrow is knockdown sexy in the way she moves, talks, and rides, and Rae Starr is determined not to get involved with this womanizing gambler. (978-1-63555-776-3)